THE GOLDEN PASTURE

THE GOLDEN PASTURE

Joyce Carol Thomas

SCHOLASTIC
HARDCOVER

Scholastic Inc.
New York

For meticulous editing, I thank
Jean Feiwel and Brenda Bowen. For love
and inspiration, I thank my aunt,
Mary Haynes Monroe, and my uncle,
Ben Monroe, still in Oklahoma,
still raising horses.
I thank my assistant, travel companion,
and sister, Flora Krasnovsky.
I thank my agent, Mitch Douglas,
for his wonderful support
and careful guidance.

No part of this publication may be reproduced in whole or in part, or
stored in a retrieval system, or transmitted in any form or by any means,
electronic, mechanical, photocopying, recording, or otherwise, without written permission of the publisher. For information regarding
permission, write to Scholastic Inc., 730 Broadway, New York, NY
10003.

Library of Congress Cataloging-in-Publication Data

Thomas, Joyce Carol.
The golden pasture.

Summary: The exquisite horse twelve-year-old Carl Lee finds on his
grandfather's farm one summer helps him to understand his difficult
father better.
        [1. Fathers and sons—Fiction. 2. Grandfathers—Fiction.
    3. Horses—Fiction. 4.Afro-Americans—Fiction] I. Title.
PZ7.T36696Go 1986   [Fic]   85-27910

ISBN 0-590-33681-9

12 11 10 9 8 7 6 5 4 3 2 1   6   6 7 8 9/8 0 1/9
                    Printed in the U.S.A.   10

I dedicate this book to my son,
Roy T. Thomas III

THERE WAS A BOY STOOD TALL IN THE WORLD on his way to becoming a man and he looked for mountains to climb and horses to tame. But there were no mountains in his part of the world, so he looked for horses to tame, and found them grazing in a golden pasture. Then he said to himself, "A mountain's a task you fix for your spirit, a wild horse the challenge to your soul." Then he looked up into the blue. To the eagle climbing the cliffs of the wind, to the hands of the sky brushing clouds across its face. To Father Time setting out the sun every morning and every evening bringing it back in. And as night fell cloaking the world in darkness, the boy decided, "I'll be that steadfast in all I begin. And if some days I fall down, if my dreams get broken, I'll dust me off, mend my dreams and start all over again, and say how lucky I am, for I am young and full of chances." There was a boy stood tall in the world on his way to becoming a man, who woke at sunrise and said, "I'll reconcile my work and leisure, pleasure, joy and duty, for if I lie down in a golden meadow, I do not waste this beauty. I bask in the wonder of mistletoe, fireflies in wheat fields, songbirds in trees, and horses who romp in these pastures. I am a young man running through high weeds, riding up tall mountains, taking my time in the climb. I have taken an oath with tomorrow and I plan to meet me there looking back at the boy standing tall in the world on his way to becoming a man."

PART I

SNOW

A CHEROKEE WOMAN, HER HEAD WRAPPED IN thick layers of red cloth, her chubby body protected by a multicolored wool coat, hurried her way through the snow.

She skipped, slowed, stopped and checked her bearings in the snow-powdered woods. These fields were so snow-powdered even the trees and shrubs and little scurrying animals wore coats of snow.

A golden-faced woman, her jet black hair hidden under the red head wrap, she moved on, aware of snow white trees, snow white bushes and snow white snow rabbits leaving little paw prints in the powder.

In places the wind had drifted the snow until it was as high as her protruding, bulging waist.

Now and then she stopped, gasped and stooped over, hands holding her belly like a basket of gold clasped close to her body.

The shawl-like fringed coat hung in such vivid colors around her that she looked like a huge peacock bird with feathers of wool skipping and stopping in the snow.

This continent of snow appeared secluded, in its own time warp, far from the cars that fled down Loganberry

Road in Ponca City, although Loganberry Road was in fact only a half a mile away from where she picked her way through the snow.

What was she looking for?

The right place.

She had to reach it in time.

The place she wanted was not an anonymous hospital bed with nurses holding thermometers and hypodermic needles. She did not want a cold stethoscope anywhere near her.

She hated the idea of the steel tools the doctor used to force a child's head out of the birth passage. She had seen the forcep marks on enough newborn babies' heads.

She wanted the child to come into the world all on its own. To have a sense of control even as early as birth.

She had not wanted Ponca City Hospital, a common place with orderlies dressed in green running in and out of her labor room.

No, she did not want to hear the sharp irritation of high-heeled shoes on the tile floors smelling like antiseptic.

Nor did she want the crackling of emergency loudspeakers calling for doctors.

She did not want the sound of death and pain and suffering anywhere near her this December day.

She had grown tired of arguing with her husband about what she didn't want when he took her to Ponca City Hospital for her checkups.

That was not the world she wanted to bring this child into.

She searched for a quiet place. A place of uncommon beauty and peace.

It was here. She had seen it many times before. She had visited this birth room which she herself had prepared.

Bent again with pain, she stopped and held onto the trunk of a pecan tree, the limbs bowed down with snow. Now a skeleton of a tree.

No, this was not the place.

She moved on.

She passed beneath a stately elm, its snow arms outstretched.

She brushed against the slender bones of honeysuckle bushes, seeing where the snow quilted the exposed branches a seamless white.

No, this was not the place. Yet.

A bushy-tailed red fox moved nearby, cunningly. He watched her.

He stayed a distance behind her and followed. Tracking her, keeping count of the times she stopped to clasp her golden belly, and the duration of each wave of pain.

The fox watched, a smile lingering just under his fox snout around his fox lips.

AT THE EDGE OF THE FOREST INTO WHICH the woman had stepped, a tall dark man almost the color of night stood wrapped in a heavy brown wool coat.

He put his hand up to his brow over which a white wool cap sat and peered off into the woods. He did not see what he wanted.

So up and down he walked, along the edge of forest, his eyes glued to the ground, searching.

He had been looking about ten minutes when he found what he had been searching for.

Tracks.

The right size.

He started running. Lightly at first. Following the tracks. Then fear squeezed his heart. And he hurried his footsteps.

Now he was panting, his breath flying in and out of his chest in great gulps and gasps.

He passed under the snow-laden pecan tree, past the Oklahoma elm, by the wild blackberry bush.

"Oh, my God," he whispered, "let me be in time."

He followed the small tracks on and on.

9

And then he heard a tiny chant lifting up through the snow air.

"Thank goodness !" he said, running on more quickly following her footsteps.

Again the snow began to fall, so quietly he didn't notice it at first. Then it was flying around his head, glueing his eyes almost shut.

He stumbled along.

The female voice hit a high piercing note just as he went flying and falling over an old pine tree stump.

"Shoot!" he fussed.

He picked himself up and forged ahead.

Soon the snow was so thick he had a time finding his way.

"Not now! Not now!" he said to the snow. But the snowflakes grew fatter, fell faster.

"Snow flurries!"

The snow covered up the woman's tracks. And the snow muffled her singing.

He pricked his ears and continued picking his way toward that song.

Then the wind blew and moaned.

He stopped because the sound of the wind covered her voice.

He trembled. "Even the wind's against me," he fussed.

He knew his woman, his wife, would not think of the noisy wind as moaning but only as Mother Nature singing and humming.

Then the wind stopped.

He pricked his ears and listened.

Now the sound of his wife singing was as pure as the newly driven snow.

It was her all right. Rose Branch Jefferson. His wife. Pregnant and alone.

What he called alone, she would call her solitude.

Ponca City Hospital where he had registered her to go for the birth where everything was safe and sanitary, she had called the last stop before you get to the funeral grounds. She could not understand birth and death being in the same building. She said.

How is it that love gets so twisted, so misunderstood. The differences in culture and background had attracted them to each other, but these differences also pulled them apart.

Then the wind started moaning again and he couldn't hear her.

He had lost her, he thought, his heart falling, but he kept on walking, hoping somehow he'd find her.

He turned to the left and soon came upon a bridge, but it was slick with ice. The bridge was a walnut wooden crossing over a frozen stream where fish hibernated under the frozen glass of the water, waiting for spring to come.

Then just on the other side of the bridge, he spotted her peacock-colored wool coat brilliant against the snow. She was stooped over near an old oak tree, probably the oldest thing in the woods, it was so large.

"Rose Branch!" he called.

Why didn't she answer?

He heard her singing muted and low. Her chanting came in gasps now, no longer like a crystal thread of music but in short notes like snippets of strings.

He could see her squatting down, her back to him, facing the tree.

11

He heard a frail cry.

The baby had come.

What was she doing bending over the child like that? He couldn't see. . . .

"Don't you kill my baby!" he hollered, alarm in his voice.

He started running across the bridge. Then he tripped and careened, sliding, skating across the treacherous ice.

He slid on his bottom, gasping from the freezing cold. He skidded until he ended up on his end on the other side of the bridge.

He picked himself up and ran to the bent-over Rose Branch, hopping through the snow the last part of the way.

She tried to cover the baby.

"You're smothering him," he yelled. He was furious at her for being out here, trying to leave him out, trying to keep him from his own child. At the same time he was excited now that he was upon her and could see it was a boy.

"Give him here!" he demanded.

The woman glared at him, but she was too weak to protest.

Besides she had to finish her job.

She bit the umbilical cord in two.

Drops of red blood on the snow white snow.

Red petals of life.

And he snatched up the child and went swooping across the snow, the child, like a little wood creature, tucked under his woolen coat and arm.

Still bleeding, Rose Branch crawled up into the hollow of the oak tree. It was dry there. She had prepared it months ago just for this time. Deer hide covered the cave. There were deer hide blankets and lots of straw to keep out the cold. It was much warmer in her cave than outside in the snowy woods. A keg of nuts and dried rust apples and dog tooth violet bulbs sat in the corner. For water, she would eat the fresh snow.

Of course she had planned to nurse her child.

From the open flap in the oak tree house, all she could see was this tall husband, moving like a crow more stealthily now, over the ice on the wooden bridge. Away from her. Her child tucked under his coat, held close to his breast, cuddled just under his heart.

She wanted to lie down in her cave and just rest. But she still had more work to do. She had to deliver the afterbirth.

She squatted again.

Inching closer, but staying out of her eye range, the sly fox watched.

Soon a wave of pain hit her and she delivered the afterbirth.

"Bury it, bury it, bury it." The old familiar chant crowded her head.

But she could not move, she was too tired from the strenuous labor and the shock of Samuel Jefferson catching her and taking the child like that.

Through heavy eyelids she saw the snow clouds part.

The sun would come out and warm the woods and melt the ice and snow on the walnut bridge.

The fox waited behind a nearby hickory tree.

When he saw this Rose Branch drifting off to sleep, he scrambled soundlessly to the tree cave, sniffing the afterbirth.

13

But Rose Branch's mother ears were so finely tuned she could distinguish the difference between a fox's feathery steps and the smallest shift in the wind.

Like any new mother, she could have heard her baby turning his head in the middle of the night.

And so she heard the fox's paw, the fox's smile and her eyes flew open.

She stared at the fox with an expression that looked beyond him and on into the next world.

The fox drooped his tail, yapped and barked, then scurried away, just a-running.

Rose Branch got up and finished her business of burying the afterbirth and reciting the chant that would protect the spirit of the child from scavengers of all kind, animal and human.

"Safe passage, safe passage along life's journey."

THE BOND

WHEN SAMUEL JEFFERSON GOT BACK TO HIS house on Loganberry Road, the entire town of Ponca showed up on his doorstep to see the baby.

Missionaries and ministers. Saints and sinners.

A little of the snow had fallen onto the infant's coal black hair and the Ponca City women, to protect him against getting chilled, bathed him in warm olive oil and gently brushed the waves of his sleek hair until it shown like blackberries or black patent leather curls.

After hearing Samuel Jefferson's story about his Cherokee wife alone out in the snowy woods, a group of Ponca women, led by Patience Jackson, went out into the forest to search for Rose Branch but they came back to sit by the warm blaze crackling in the fireplace, saying they could not find her.

During the next few days, nursing women, who were still breastfeeding their own babies, took turns nursing the infant born in the woods.

Samuel Jefferson's Ponca City neighbors were so generous, he didn't need to buy a thing. The women brought old and new baby clothes by.

A few days later, when bottles of mother's milk started

16

appearing on his doorstep, he assumed the nursing women had expressed milk from their breasts and left the bottles there.

When he thanked the Ponca women, they stared at him blankly. He chalked it all up to that community pride those women had such an abundance of. Why thank them when they considered it their duty?

"What are you going to call him?" asked Patience Jackson one day. She was a plump brown-skinned woman, pretty and practical.

Patience had recently married Strong Jackson. Of all the Ponca City women, she had been the most consistent and diligent visitor to the Jefferson house.

Her husband Strong understood her need to help. They had been busy trying to get Patience pregnant. In fact, she was sure she had just conceived. If her calculations were right, then she'd have the baby in September.

She went about with a secret smile of knowing, thinking about the possibility of her own child as she practiced motherhood on this baby boy, changing his diapers, burping him after he finished his milk.

"I don't know," Samuel Jefferson finally responded to her question about a name. He thought of naming the baby after his father, but he and his father, Grayson Jefferson, hadn't seen eye to eye in a long, long time.

"Well, do like the old folks used to do. Wait until you have a sign," said Patience, rocking the baby boy, swaddled in baby blue blankets, back and forth.

After heeding what Patience had said, he looked for signs, but he didn't see any.

His father would have called him blind. There were signs all around him.

Sun was peeking through the December clouds one morning when he picked up the milk bottle left again outside his front door.

Later that day, when he poured the last drop from the large milk bottle into the smaller baby bottle, he noticed this etching on the big bottle's bottom: The Carlton Bottling Company.

"That's his name. Carlton," said Jefferson. "Well, Carlton sounds too plain. Carlton Lee. That's it. Carlton Lee. Carlton Lee Jefferson."

He finally wrote his father, sent the letter off to Golden Pasture where his father's ranch was. "Dear Pa, you finally have that grandson you wanted so bad. His name is Carlton Lee Jefferson. I hope you're proud. Your son, Samuel Jefferson."

Over in Golden Pasture, Gray Jefferson finished watering and grooming his horses.

Before he knew it it was time to meet the mail rider.

It was a distance to the mailboxes and since he had a few items to pick up in town anyway, he jumped in his truck and must have reached the gate just after the mail rider left, for there was a letter waiting. The red flag was up.

Leaving the motor running, he took the letter out of the box and let the red flag back down.

He shut the gate and got back into the truck.

Immediately he opened the envelope from his son. When he read the letter's short message, a curious smile crossed his face and he said, "Well now."

18

The thick-haired, clean-shaven Gray sat the letter on the seat beside him. Then he stuck his mighty hands on the gear shift, moved into third gear and sped the truck along the gravel road until he intersected the Oklahoma Highway.

He didn't stop in town at all. He just kept on coming. He drove on into Ponca City to see this Carlton Lee Jefferson.

Around noon, Gray pulled up to the small wood house, white now because it was covered with December snow, and parked his truck.

He took giant leaps across the snowy lawn and banged on the door before entering.

He spoke quickly to his son, Samuel, and headed for the baby crib.

He leaned over, unwrapped the baby blankets and examined his grandson from head to toe.

"Why he's grinning at me. I believe he knows who I am," said Gray, rubbing the blackberry curls on the baby's head. "And he's got a dimple in his chin just like mine," he exclaimed proudly.

He wrapped the child back up.

With his tall frame, he looked like some wonderful brown giant hanging over the crib and tickling the cleft of Carl Lee's chin.

"Oh, look at him smile," said Gray.

"That's just a ghost smile," said Patience Jackson, over in the corner near the stove ironing baby clothes. Hadn't she heard the older women talking about the angels playing around the corners of babies' mouths?

Gray Jefferson paid no mind to that. His grandson was different.

And every time Gray spoke, the baby grinned.

Samuel Jefferson proceeded to act jealous.

"You heard what the woman said," Samuel growled. "'It's just a ghost smile.'"

"Of course I heard what she said, but I also know what I'm looking at," said Gray.

At the sound of Gray's voice, Carlton Lee smiled again.

"Where's the child's mama?" said Gray.

"She disappeared. Probably died off in the woods somewhere. Must have been suffering from childbirth-sickness. When I found her, she was trying to smother this poor critter."

Gray, not believing that last part, glared at his son. "She'd still be home if you'd treated her right."

"Now don't you come in my house starting any confusion, old man. This is my house!"

"I still say that Indian woman would still be here if you knew how to cooperate sometimes and learned how to show a little affection. Black folks and Cherokees have been marrying and getting along for as long as I can remember. It's worked for centuries, what's your problem?"

"Out of my house. Out!" screamed Samuel.

At the sound of his daddy's quarreling voice little Carlton Lee started squawling.

"See what you've gone and done," said Gray, picking the baby up and whispering to him. "Now, now, Carl Lee, my little Carl Lee."

The baby hushed.

Patience Jackson who had opened her mouth to ask the men to quit fussing out of regard for the child said,

"Well, shut my mouth!" she was so amazed at the newborn's response. She couldn't wait to tell the women in the Ponca City quilting bee about this smart baby who knew his own grandfather's voice from anybody else's.

Samuel Jefferson didn't say another fuming word. He too just stood in awe of the magic Gray Jefferson had worked with the baby, Carl Lee.

Sometimes love plays games. It leaps and hopscotches over the heads of fathers and sons and matches up fathers and grandsons.

Such was the case with Gray and Carlton Lee.

And when her ironing was done, Patience Jackson rushed off to tell the amazing news: a baby boy born in the snow, coming into the world already acquainted with his own grandpa.

At last when Gray kissed Carl Lee's brow and finished cooing over him like an old woman, he reluctantly jumped in his pickup and headed down Loganberry Road on his way to the highway that led to Golden Pasture.

When the door closed behind Gray, Carl Lee started crying, crying his heart out, as though he felt his grandfather had abandoned him to his own father.

Samuel Jefferson picked up his son and rocked him, suspecting there was a bond between grandfather and grandson that would never ever be broken.

PART II

KING OF THE HORSES

IN GOLDEN PASTURE LATE ONE THURSDAY afternoon, twelve-year-old Carl Lee bent over the sink at his grandfather's kitchen window preparing lemonade and looking out the window onto the backyard.

He watched Gray and Billingsley carving hickory wood statues in the half shade of a blackjack tree. Billingsley was Gray's best friend. A rodeo partner from the good old days.

As he squeezed the lemons in the glass pitcher he thought his grandfather and Billingsley looked like two old benign buzzards, with their backs humped by time.

Carl Lee was a thin boy, with warm brown eyes offset by thick bushy eyebrows looking like two black wings.

His skin was clay brown. There was a dimple in his chin.

And when girls looked at his hair they thought of peppercorns and blackberries.

He stirred honey into the lemon juice then added water.

"Who would have thought," Carl Lee said softly to himself, thinking of a time when Gray and Billingsley's backs were straighter, when they sat taller in the saddle and rode fifty to a hundred miles a day in the thick heat of Oklahoma hills and New Mexico mountains rounding up wild horses for the Boley Rodeo.

According to stories his grandfather told him, the horses ran, hysterical with rage, galloping over prairie grass, up and down gulleys, stamping up red dirt clouds, unsettling clay dust, jackknifing, kicking holes out of the ground, trying to escape the roundup.

He turned to the refrigerator to add ice to the lemonade, still listening to the voices of the older men.

"Yessir, we rounded up some bad horses for the Boley Rodeo, all right," his grandfather was saying.

Gray Jefferson, dressed in a pair of blue overalls and a denim shirt, scraped at the wooden figurine he sculpted. He was so tall, his head barely cleared the blackjack tree he sat under. A big man, husky even though his back was stooped just a little bit. The more than twelve years since Carl Lee had been born had aged him. Now he was grizzly-bearded, a white halo of hair sticking out around his head. Hands, gnarled knobby with age but still heavy with power.

"Remember that four-legged scoundrel, Broken Bones?" said Billingsley.

"Broken Bones? Do I remember? Who could forget? Went beyond his name. That mustang broke bones all right, but he didn't stop there. Broke bones and backs!" hooted Gray.

"What year was it he tore down the corral, wrecked a car, broke rail fences over the rider's back, and sent that poor cowboy out on a stretcher?"

"Any year he came, he cut up. He didn't have any special time for acting up. You've got to have crickets in

27

your chimney to climb up on anybody's wild New Mexico mountain horse."

"Yet we lived to tell it."

"Still . . . ain't nothing like the Boley Rodeo," said Gray. "You can raise hell in peace."

"Remember the year that Thunderfoot. . . ?"

"Who wouldn't?"

"Horse never should have been caught and sent to the rodeo," said Billingsley.

"He's. . . . " Gray halted as Carl Lee appeared.

"Lemonade, just the ticket for a dry gullet," Gray said, accepting the ice-crackling pitcher. As he wiped the sweat from under his hat band, he added, "Heard the palomino calling you, Carl Lee."

"I think he wants to be saddled, Grandpa."

"Either that or he's having a bad day. Horses, like people, do have bad days, you know. Maybe he's feeling cranky with a headache."

"A headache? You mean horses have headaches too?"

"They have heads don't they?"

"Big heads," said Carl Lee.

"Big headaches."

Carl Lee said, "My lands," then stretched out on his back under the redbud tree next to the porch where he could relax in the shade and watch the grasshoppers springing and krickety-kricking across the buffalo grass, thinking about what size aspirin a horse would have to take. "The size of a plate," he imagined.

The palomino called again.

He had promised his grandfather he'd be able to recite "There Was a Boy" before he rode again. Gray had

28

taught him not to break promises. "A man's word is his bond."

How did the poem go? Under his breath he recited, "There was a boy stood tall in the world on his way to becoming a man, and he looked for mountains to climb and wild horses to tame. But there were no mountains in his part of the world, so he looked for wild horses to tame, and found them grazing in a golden pasture. Then he said to himself, 'A mountain's a task you fix for your spirit, a wild horse the challenge to your soul.' Then he looked . . . . looked . . . ." He couldn't remember the rest.

Out loud he said, "You know something, Grandpa, if I had my way, they'd conduct school in a yellow pasture and compute arithmetic problems on horseback."

"Be kind of hard on the teacher, don't you think?" said Gray whittling away at his stick of hickory wood.

Carl Lee said, "If I could trade places with the math instructor I'd compose problems asking for the circumference of a corral, the area of a horse's stall, the number of meters from the stable to the house."

Carl Lee' s mind drifted and in his dreamworld he listened to the rhythm of the southern drawl coloring and seasoning all his grandfather's and Billingsley's words.

He liked to hear these two heroes talk their old fogey talk as he called it, for their voices were as rich as a country landscape and ripe with stories.

His grandfather, who came to Oklahoma by way of Mississippi, had a storehouse of Mississippi stories about alligators, and Oklahoma stories about Indians and horses and rodeos.

Carl Lee especially enjoyed hearing about the black cowboys and the Boley Rodeo. He had wanted to ride in the Boley Rodeo for as long as he could remember. But each year Gray said he was too young, too inexperienced. Everybody knew you had to be thirteen. And that was an exception, most folks didn't ride until they were fifteen years old. Old men, thought Carl Lee.

But Carl Lee was anxious to prove himself. He couldn't wait any longer. Thirteen was half a year away. An eternity. And next summer he'd be thirteen and a half, already an older man when the Boley Rodeo rolled around again.

He wanted to perfect some horse tricks but the palomino was too tame for the rodeo. Didn't have a lick of spirit.

He couldn't figure out yet just what he could do. He wanted to participate in the rodeo this Labor Day. Do something so wonderful they'd have to call him "cowboy" instead of "cowpoke."

But the palomino was too tame.

The late sun was making him doze.

He'd never figure out anything lazying around like this. But he closed his eyes anyway.

His grandfather's sidekick startled him out of a daze by tapping him on the shoulder and handing him the thing he had sculpted. "Here's a saddle, son," said Billingsley.

Then his grandfather showed him the hickory horse. The saddle fit just right.

"Why, thanks," he said lifting himself up off the ground. "Better quit kicking against bricks and go inside and study!"

THAT THURSDAY AFTER SCHOOL, CARL LEE, astride the palomino, trotted along the road toward home, accompanied by his two school friends, Jessie and Norman who rode their palominos, one on each side of Carl Lee.

"You know something, Carl Lee, I heard my folks say your grandpa keeps a secret horse in the stalls somewhere," said Jessie, one hand up trying to keep his big hat from swallowing his narrow head. "They say the horse came from Arabia or some place strange like that."

"I heard the same story," said the tobacco-colored Norman. "And they say if you listen closely, at three o'clock in the morning you can hear the sound of your grandfather and that secret horse galloping over the earth where there aren't any fences. Hooves pounding like drums."

"How do you know it's a horse?" said Carl Lee. "Maybe it's some other wild animal they're talking about."

"Nothing sounds like a horse running but a horse running," said Jessie.

"Now that's the truth," Carl Lee admitted, looking at the palomino he rode not only to school but every chance he could get, sometimes even from the house to the barn.

"I heard it myself," said Norman in a quiet voice.

"Heard what?" said Jessie.

"The secret horse."

Carl Lee and Jessie turned to look at him.

Norman had a strange sound in his voice. He said, "Once I stayed up late one night just to see if I could hear Gray Jefferson riding that secret horse. I heard something, but when I looked out the window I didn't see a thing except the moon. It was a funny feeling, looking at the moon and hearing that galloping sound and not being able to see horse nor rider. It was a quiet night except for that.

"It was clear and the moon was full. There was something strange in the air. A funny, funny feeling," said Norman.

"Funny feelings? I know exactly what you mean," said Carl Lee. "I get one when I look at the No Trespassing sign in that forsaken corner of our ranch."

"What's that?" his friends chimed in unison.

"Certain off limits areas on the ranch," said Carl Lee.

"Off limits?"

"Anyway nobody goes back there," said Carl Lee, catching himself and wanting to change the subject. Maybe he had talked too much.

Carl Lee chewed on a blade of alfalfa grass and studied the golden coat and silvery mane of his palomino. He didn't want to talk too much about his grandfather's business. But already, he could see his own curiosity mirrored in the eyes of his two friends.

32

Norman said, "My grandpa says your grandpa's the best cowboy in the county. And I never heard him compliment anybody before in my whole life. In fact, nothing I do can please him. He's the orneriest old cuss in Oklahoma."

Jessie said, "My grandpa's just the opposite. I can't do a thing to get him mad. I have tried him. Nothing. I can't raise even a growl from him."

"How'd you like my grandpa's knuckles upside your head? That grayheaded son-of-a-gun's got hands like rocks," said Norman.

"At least you know what the parameters are. You know what I mean?" said Jessie.

"What's this big word, parameters?" asked Carl Lee.

"Oh, he heard it in his social living class. One way parents and grandparents show love is by demanding that the adolescent act in a responsible manner. 'Letting you teenagers know what your responsibilities are,'" he said sounding just like a teacher. "Stuff like that. Those are the parameters."

"Hey, you got it. Almost word for word, Norm," said Jessie.

"I haven't had that class yet," said Carl Lee.

"You will," they assured him.

"My grandpa's parameters are his heavy hands," said Norman.

Carl Lee nervously brushed at his blackberry hair. "Your grandpa sounds like my father," he said to Norman. "Mean."

They paced slowly ahead, silently thinking about parents and grandparents and growing up.

Parameters, Carl Lee thought, is that what he was missing from his own father? His father's parameters were set by cursing, swearing, and threatening.

Ever since Carl Lee had reached adolescence, the relationship with his father had become more strained.

Almost as though his father feared something. But what? That Carl Lee was almost a teenager? A sure sign he was growing up, becoming a man? Maybe his daddy wanted him to stay a baby. He had been nicer when Carl Lee was younger.

"My mama's dead," Carl Lee said to his friends. "She died when I was born."

"Oh, man," said Jessie. "I can't imagine not having my mama."

"Me either," Norman said.

"I know," said Carl Lee.

Carl Lee longed for a mother, like everybody else had.

Still he wasn't an orphan. It would be hard to be an orphan in a place like Ponca City where the neighbors knew your every move.

"Count your blessings," his grandfather had said, and that command echoed in his head every time he wanted to feel sorry for himself.

"I'm no whiner," he decided.

When boys got past twelve, they pretended their tear ducts had dried up.

But sometimes at night their tears still flowed. However, none of them ever talked about this.

Instead they said, "You know that Alex down yonder on Deer Creek Road? He's the biggest crybaby you ever did see."

"Alex is always looking for something to cry about."
It was all right to be a crybaby but not where people could see you.

"Yeah, you know he's going to tune up and cry when his chin drops. Face so long he could put a bridle on it and eat oats out of a churn. Saw him yesterday weeping about having to milk the cows at four in the morning. That high-behinded boy might not ever grow up!" said Norman.

"Either that or he's gonna turn into a girl. High behind and all."

They were silent. That was one of their greatest fears, to turn into a girl!

They thought about it every time they cried like a girl at night in their private beds.

"You know something," said Carl Lee, following their unspoken line of thought, "my grandfather says it's all right to cry sometimes."

"He did?!"

"Sure did. Said many's the day he's cried like a baby, and he's sure he'll be crying about one thing or another if he gets to be a hundred. The world can be a sad, sad place, according to him."

"Well, nothing womanish about that old cowboy," said Jessie.

"No, my grandfather doesn't have to apologize about anything," said Carl Lee.

"That must be the way to live," said Norman. "Not too many 'I'm sorry's.' And no backing up in your life. Cry if you feel like it. But laugh most of the time."

"Any time you got family in the world, you're going

to have some crying days, that's what my Grandpa claims," said Carl Lee.

"I see him in church every Sunday but I'd like to really meet him, sit down and talk to him," said Jessie.

"Me, too, when are you going to invite us over?" asked Norman.

"I don't know," said Carl Lee, thinking. He liked having his grandfather to himself. Always when he was at home with his dad, he got no attention except an awful lot of fussing from his father about the sloppy way he washed dishes, or the five or six blades of grass he missed with the lawn mower. His father didn't like him asking a lot of questions either.

Asking questions. That was Carl Lee's favorite pastime. When he was three and four he drove his father crazy asking, "Where does the wind go when it blows away? What color is a thought? And Daddy, where do mamas go when they die?"

Asking questions, looking for answers. And the next door neighbors let him be an unofficial part of their family of nine kids. But next door he was just one among many. And with nine kids they didn't have time to answer all his questions. They could barely keep up with questions from their own flock. So he stopped asking.

Sometimes his grandfather answered questions he didn't even know he had.

At his grandfather's he could ask as many questions as he wanted.

At his grandfather's he was king of the horses.

"I don't know," Carl Lee said to his friends again, not wanting to sound mean and selfish. "I'll let you know."

"Hey, Carl Lee, I'd like to come and hike in that No Trespassing pasture," said Jessie.

"Me too," said Norman.

"No way. Grandpa wouldn't like it," said Carl Lee.

"Don't you ever wonder what's back there?" they asked Carl Lee. "How can you stand not knowing?"

Carl Lee just shrugged; they had come to the entrance to his grandfather's ranch. He turned his horse off the main road.

"Well, I guess I'd better be moseying on along," he said. "See you."

His friends and their horses soon disappeared in the distance. He headed his horse along the fence until he came to the wooden bridge that crossed Opal Lake. As always, he tightened the reins so the palomino would stop.

Today the lake air thickened with the croaking of bug-eyed frogs and the noisy quack-quack of the ducks that lived in this blue lagoon stretching the entire length of his grandfather's forty acres.

Opal Lake, fed by an underground spring, flowed as clear and iridescent as the lights in an opal. Water plants floated on the crystal stream and long-beaked birds haunted the surface for the little water bugs forever skipping across its top.

On the shore, a mallard duck craned her long brown neck at her brood and the ducklings flexed their webbed feet, lifted their thin, reedlike legs higher and waddled after their mother into the swimming stream.

All the ducks on Opal Lake were just losing their flight feathers which fell away on the shore and in the stream. But the most dramatic change affected the drakes, the glorious male ducks with the iridescent colors, who dropped their rainbow feathers in the water, their bodies signaling summer by copying the ordinary brown of the female.

Carl Lee dismounted and walked down to the water. He picked up two floating colorful drake feathers, stuck one in his cowboy hat and carried the other back up to the bridge to his horse. He placed this one on his horse's saddle, then continued along the fence until he came to his grandfather's gate.

CLOP-CLOP, CLOP-CLOP. THE PALOMINO paused for a moment at the mailbox that marked the place the path turned, then moved on, proudly swishing his golden tail and wearing the glorious drake feather Carl Lee had fished out of Opal Lake. There was no sweeter sound on earth as far as Carl Lee was concerned than the sound of horses' hooves beating against the earth. A perfect rhythm.

Such grace, such balance. He even liked the way horses held their heads.

Soon Carl Lee and the palomino came to the part of the gravel path that branched to the house and then veered off on to the barn.

The ranch house, made of red bricks compressed from Oklahoma red clay, stood on a small rising. The brick fortress, shaded by southern pines, looked secure and as though it had stood there forever.

"He's home," Carl Lee sighed with relief, seeing his grandfather's Ford pickup parked at the end of the driveway. A little way from the house stood the barn made of wood. And every summer, they whitewashed it.

Beyond the trained plants of the enclosed ranch yard,

39

beyond the leaning picket fence, the mesquite and sagebrush expanded his view. Untamed buffalo grass and wire weeds carpeted the way to the horse stables. And the warm wind brought him the raunchy, sweaty rich odor of horses, musky and compelling.

He led the horse between the house, past the vegetable garden of okra, greens, tomatoes, peas, corn and toward the barn.

"Whoa," he said.

He dismounted and stabled the horse in the barn.

He let out to pasture the two cows which supplied enough milk, butter, cream and buttermilk that they never had to buy dairy products from the store.

For a moment he stood and watched the cows slowly roam the fields, their cowbells clanking gently.

Walking back to the house on the other side of the barn he passed the chicken coop fenced in with chicken wire circling the yard for the chickens and roosters and the three turkeys that strutted and gobbled there.

Even before he could reach the house, he knew what they were having for dinner. The aroma was unmistakable: pinto beans. And if they were having pinto beans that meant hot buttered cornbread to go with it. And maybe a gallon of loganberry juice to wash it down. Early spinach from the garden made into a crisp salad.

The only thing he was never sure of was dessert. He couldn't smell it cooking. It was always fresh fruit, finished off with a glass of milk. And his grandfather was full of surprises. Once they had fresh cantaloupes and it was too early for cantaloupes. His grandfather had gone all the way to Langston to a special produce market to find the round, luscious fruit. Mexican cantaloupes.

His grandfather was as unpredictable as a Mexican cantaloupe on an Oklahoma table at Christmas.

This lazy June day, he was thinking about how wonderfully unpredictable his grandfather was as he dashed up the front porch steps and opened the screen door.

The living room testified to the fact that there was no woman within miles of the ranch. This front room was solid and comfortable. Hardwood floor but no rugs. Knotty pine walls that needed no painting. A brick fireplace. An old stuffed sofa, kind of a green color and lumpy, absolutely perfect for kicking off the boots and lounging. There were no little starched doilies on the sofa back or sofa arm to worry about sliding off and onto the floor. And no fluffy laced pillows that could only be used to look at.

Across from the sofa sat a rocking chair that his grandfather liked to sit in and read his paper and think and watch television. A brass floor lamp for light stood like a sentry next to the rocking chair and two end tables of oak wood sat on each end of the sofa.

"Grandpa," Carl Lee called, "I'm home."

"I've been in the kitchen, carrying on with the pots and pans," Gray boomed, coming into the living room. "How was school?"

"So-so," came Carl Lee's usual answer.

"Well, horse," one of Gray's fond names for Carl Lee, "want a snack before you get started on the chores and homework?"

"Maybe something to hold me before dinner," he said, putting his backpack of books down on the lumpy green couch and following his grandfather to the kitchen.

The no-nonsense kitchen went with the living room. It was practical, including in its simple design a white Wedgewood stove, a Sears and Roebuck white refrigerator and ample counter space.

This cooking and eating room repeated the walls of knotty pine seen in the living room. Pots and pans hung down from the ceiling and a sturdy oak table and chairs sat in the center of the green linoleum floor.

"Something to hold you before dinner," Gray chuckled. "That's what I thought you'd say. We've got left-over potato salad, and," he opened the refrigerator with a flourish, "the makings of a rodeo sandwich."

A rodeo sandwich was anything you could round up to put between two slices of bread.

Gray reached in the refrigerator and pulled out a boiled egg, a yellow chunk of cheese, lettuce, tomatoes, sliced beef left over from a Sunday roast and one solitary fried chicken drumstick. He sliced and piled all this onto the bread and made Carl Lee an enormous sandwich. So big it was a chore to wrap the lips around the whole thing. Then he made one for himself. Just as hearty.

They ate with Carl Lee talking between bites and swallows about the assignments Miss Monroe had given him for the English class, memorizing that long, long poem due by the end of the summer session and writing an essay called "How I Think Golden Pasture Got Its Name." The essay was due right away.

"I wonder how she thinks up all these memorization and writing exercises," said Carl Lee.

"That's her job," said Gray.

"And what did you do today?" asked Carl Lee after draining his glass of ice cold milk.

"Same old, same old, groomed the horses, mended a few fences, started dinner, talked to Billingsley."

Carl Lee didn't consider Billingsley competition the way he considered his younger friends, Norman and Jessie. I'm the only young person I want my grandfather paying attention to, he thought. Billingsley was too old to be anything but comfortable around.

Carl Lee glowed with happiness. Summers with his grandfather were the grandest times of all.

He walked to the white-washed barn and began his evening chores.

He rubbed down the five horses, swept out the barn, spread the straw out in the stalls, evenly. And went to the well, a well that drew its water from the same underground crystal spring that swelled Opal Lake.

He let down the bucket and lifted up the coolest, sweetest water in Oklahoma. Using the tin dipper that had hung on the well wall for generations, he drank a long draft then carried the bucket back and forth from the well to the animals' troughs, watching the fuzzy-tongued cows lap up the cool water until their thirst was slaked and there was water to spare.

He enjoyed the country so much he thought the chores were a new kind of fun.

Maybe it was the way his grandfather set things up. He wasn't sure.

Even Gray's lectures turned out to be stories and fairy tales. He didn't know anybody who was as lucky as he was when it came to grandfathers.

When the chores were finished, he started to his room to study before dinner. In the living room, he picked up his books off the lumpy green couch.

His grandfather was relaxing in his rocking chair chuckling and reading *The Golden Pasture Gazette*.

"Great day in the morning!" he said rustling the paper as Carl Lee walked past on his way to his room. "Listen to this. A man divorcing his wife said he wanted the house and all the horses. Claimed the woman was too citified. He caught her a rabbit and asked her to cook it. And she asked, 'But how do I get the feathers off?!' He said he should have known something was strange when right after the honeymoon she took a bucket and went out in the barn to milk the horses.

"Not many women left like your grandma, that woman could do anything," claimed Gray.

Carl Lee looked over at his grandmother's picture.

She had died before he was born. The photograph was one of those where the eyes followed you around the room. And she had a hint of a bittersweet smile on her chocolate lips as if she listened to the conversation too.

"She sure was beautiful, Grandpa," he said admiring her picture with the black wooly hair brushed neatly into two spirally buns twisted to the side of her head above two perfect ears.

"By the way," Carl Lee said turning back around, "did the man get the house and the horses?"

"No," said Gray, folding up the paper. "The woman got the horses and the man got the house. You tell me, is that justice?"

"Now that would make a good writing assignment," said Carl Lee, turning to go down the hallway to his room.

"Remember what I told you, Carl Lee," said Gray.

44

"Jot your ideas down. Or else those words will grow wings and just fly away. You know it's the lead in the pencil that puts an anchor on thoughts. They're not liable to get up so easy and run away. Why words are just like horses, harness them on the page. Claim them."

"Oh, grandpa," Carl Lee chuckled.

"All right, I'm telling you," said Gray good-naturedly. "Imagine how you'll feel if a thought you had flies to somebody else's head. Next thing you know some other student's claimed it and gets the credit, just because he's had the good sense and foresight to write it down."

With Gray's words ringing in his head, Carl Lee continued down the hall.

His room included a bed with a mattress like a rock. "Boys need firmness for their backbones," Gray had claimed.

A small table and chair that served as a desk sat under a window looking out over the pasture. In the corner across from the desk stood a chest of drawers with an oval mirror hanging above it.

Everything in the room was blue. A blue bedspread, a blue hooked rug and blue walls.

Horse pictures he had found in magazines decorated the walls.

As he sat at his desk covered with several scratch pads, a mug of pencils and pens, he thought he'd get started on Miss Monroe's composition first. She was always expecting the best. And nobody liked to see her frown. When she frowned the whole classroom got dim. She had said they were to write a short essay on how they thought Golden Pasture got its name. "Make up something," she had said. "It doesn't have to be true."

He picked up his pencil. Opened the composition book. But he didn't write anything. He sat still and let his mind wander.

He kept thinking about the name "Golden Pasture." How to get a golden pasture in summer. Maybe plant alfalfa in row after row. The kind that produce yellow flowers.

He started jotting down his ideas on a piece of yellow scratch paper.

Bury yellow iris bulbs?

Scatter daisies?

Or design a field of goldenrod.

Wait! Plant something as common as daffodils.

To get a golden pasture let the buffalo grass, mowed and sickled, collect the Oklahoma sun.

He looked out his bedroom window over the fields and fields of alfalfa. He knew this variety would give acres and acres of yellow flowers as the summer progressed, but there was also another way to get gold from alfalfa.

He wrote "alfalfa" on the next line of his yellow pad.

Once the alfalfa was ready to be cut and dried, he knew they would bale it. Then leave the stacks in the fields to dry.

When all of this became hay, he would look out over the meadow and see the haystacks of gold.

This possibility from common straw excited him.

Oh, but let the sun hit straw, it turns to gold. And the smell of gold is honeysuckle or the aroma of hay when it's kissed by the sun.

He said to himself, You are lucky if you take off your

boots and stand barefoot, your toes tickled by the straw, in the midst of a golden pasture.

"I'll keep that part," he whispered, scribbling down the thought on his scratch paper.

His mind kept traveling back to what Gray had said. Thoughts have wings, if you don't put them down they fly away to the next person. Why one day you might hear some other student standing up in the classroom reading something you thought. Jot things down. That's what Gray had told him. It was supposed to be a joke. But Carl Lee wondered if it really was.

He went back to thinking about Golden Pasture.

He would pretend the town of Golden Pasture got its name from the yellow flowers of alfalfa plants and the stacks of hay in the Oklahoma fields.

Every writing assignment starts in the mind first, Miss Monroe said. Now all he had to do was organize his notes and thoughts on paper.

Then he'd read this draft to his grandfather who always listened with a smile on his lips.

He started writing, "You're lucky if you ever get the chance to take off your boots and stand barefoot in a golden pasture and let the hay tickle your toes. That's what the founder of Golden Pasture did when he saw the wild alfalfa fields blooming like gold all over Oklahoma as far as he could see. . . ."

It was easy. All he had to do was put the words down until one word followed the other. Until the words faithfully echoed his thoughts.

Once he got started, he said to himself, this could be fun, even if he did hate summer school.

"Thank God, it's Friday," he whispered after writing a page worth on Golden Pasture.

He closed his composition book, laced his hands behind his head and looked out over the fields.

At last his eye settled on the No Trespassing sign.

"How can you stand not knowing?" His friends' question echoed in his head.

Well, it wasn't the easiest thing in the world. Many's the time he wanted to strike out over to the No Trespassing pasture anyway.

But his grandfather might turn into somebody like Norman's grandfather. He didn't ever want to experience Gray's heavy hands.

It wasn't the hands that scared him, it was Gray's being upset with him. His stomach churned just thinking about it.

Through the window that No Trespassing sign beaconed at him like an odd-colored string of rodeo lights dressed up in neon.

It might as well have said, "Come on."

He wouldn't. The only thing stopping him was the frown he knew would cross Gray's face.

With a father like he had he didn't need his grandfather against him too.

Sitting at this open window he heard the quack-quack of a drake calling to a duck and her ducklings down by Opal Lake.

"The grandfather wind is stirring," he said.

When it blew, even slightly, he could hear duck and frog sounds from the lake more clearly. And the wind, older than memory, puffed his cheeks and blew the fragrance of the southern pines that swayed over the brick house so gently yet so resolutely that the pine scent wafted through the bricks and sifted through his open window. Pine perfumed the air, reminding him of other aromas.

He remembered two distinct scents: the smell of his father's anger and the fresh fruit aroma of the apple woman.

That musky combination happened a long time ago, but the memory came back to him through his senses.

"Who?" his father had said to him years ago. He could remember the incident just as plain, as plain as the nose on his face and the smell in his mind.

"The apple woman," Carl Lee had said.

"I told you there's no such person, how many times do I have to tell you that?"

"There is. She smells like apples, and she looks like a golden goddess!"

Samuel's ears perked. "You dreamed it."

"I didn't."

"What does a golden . . . goddess look like?"

"Look like? Oh, Daddy she's got skin like gold. Gold bird feathers stuck in her black hair. Gold glass beads around her neck. Daddy, gold shimmering bracelets up her arm."

"Where'd you see her?"

Carl Lee giggled with joy, thinking, *My Daddy's talking to me*. This was the first time in a long while Samuel had asked him questions and listened so intently to him. *Oh, we're actually talking*.

"At my window. I saw her at my window."

"When?"

"Sometimes when I wake up. The smell of apples

comes through my window and there she is," he piped in his little boy's voice. "An arm full of apples. I watch as she eats them."

"Didn't she offer you any?"

"Yes, but you told me never to take food from a stranger."

"That's right," said Samuel, a troubling shadow piercing his eye. "But you dreamed it. You dreamed the whole thing," he whispered; however, his whisper was a hoarse shout that got lower and louder.

Catching this tension in his own voice, Samuel forced patience in his tone. "Sometimes when we're waking up in the morning we get our dreams and our real world all mixed up. You see, Carl Lee, I'm real. I'm the most real thing in your life."

Carl Lee stopped giggling, sorry he'd ever told Samuel about the golden woman and the essence of apples.

Then his dream and reality really did get mixed up.

He flinched remembering the last time he saw the goddess.

She came and stood by his window, her arms filled with rust apples, a smile lingering softly around her golden mouth; something else invaded the air of the dream.

He smelled it first as a scorched stench that over-whelmed the familiar apple aroma. Sweat. The acid scent of anger.

Then he heard it. A shouting at the window. The golden goddess' smile turned inside out.

Her weeping jerked him upright in bed.

He jumped up to go to her aid.

50

But when his feet hit the floor, the only person standing at his window was his father.

"See, I told you," Samuel had said. "There's nobody here. See. There's nobody here but me. And a bird or two," all the time picking up the golden feathers off the ground below the window. He kept saying this: "Nobody here but me."

Now, sitting at his grandfather's window looking out at the No Trespassing sign, Carl Lee let the scent of pine replace the remarkable aromas he remembered.

He shivered. He couldn't figure out why there was so much pain in the recollection of that long ago morning, yet he could not conjure up that last encounter without concluding that somehow his father had kept his dream from him by running it away.

Time to rest that memory and think of something else, he sighed to himself.

No Trespassing indeed.

Then he turned away from this pair of windows: away from the window with the sign beckoning him and especially away from the memory window in his mind.

"Better halter that horse and harness another one!" he spoke, so loud he startled himself and any golden witness who might have been listening.

NO TRESPASSING

"MAIL RIDER'S COME AND GONE," CARL LEE said spying the red flag sticking up on the mailbox.

His sinking voice echoed so low, his horse whinnied.

When his jean-wet thighs involuntarily clamped tighter around the palomino, the horse shivered.

The mailbox, waiting on wooden legs, was a sign post for the path that led to the ranch house. The box, carved in the shape of a horse, bowed its dull head under the heat wave as though it had something even hotter in its belly.

Trying to delay what he might discover inside, Carl Lee slowly lowered the red wooden flag shaped like a horse's ear.

As he reached for the flap that opened the gray mouth of the box, he mumbled, "Probably another threatening letter."

Sweat poured from his forehead until his face glistened as wet as his clothes, still dripping from his swim in Opal Lake.

At least three times a week his father sent a letter to Gray in Golden Pasture threatening to pick up Carl Lee, claiming he needed his son in Ponca City to look after the house, as though the house were a person.

Carl Lee opened the mailbox.

Anxiety dizzied him until his ears rang and he couldn't see right. Water in his ears. Shadows in the mailbox. And in the center of the darkness a sharp rectangular white-hot stone.

The horse stood perfectly still.

A butterfly landed on the horse's ear and he quivered the ear and swished his palomino tail. The sound broke the spell and Carl Lee could hear the crickets again. And his eyes cleared.

Now he could make out the white envelope all right.

He grabbed the letter from the box and raked his glance across the handwriting.

"Doggone it!" he said to the horse. "Why can't he leave us alone this one summer."

Last summer his visit had been cut short by five weeks when Samuel swooped down and dragged him away from chores in the barn and fields, leaving the horses and cows unfed and the water bucket overturned in the pasture.

Quickly, Carl Lee stuck the letter in his wet shirt pocket.

Realizing his mistake, he yanked it out, but it was too late. The letter was soppy wet with the ink lines all running together.

"Can't read this anyhow," Carl Lee said. Furiously, he tore the soaked letter to pieces and chucked the whole mess in the bushes.

His father never wrote directly to Carl Lee. He talked

around him, about him in letters to Gray, but rarely directly to his own son. Carl Lee resented that.

Many times Carl Lee'd thought of throwing the letters away, hating to see the frown that crossed Gray's face as he would read the disturbing messages.

For a moment, it felt good, tearing that letter up like that.

He thought, My father is like the winter. Why I can't even remember the last time I saw him laugh. A face all torn up like a tornado. A smile dead as the alfalfa grass in winter. A spirit buried under the pine tree ground.

As he got closer to the house, he saw the familiar Ford. "On no, Daddy's here," he whispered.

Soon he heard the dreadful sound of quarreling. Trouble. "Whoa," he whispered. He pulled on the reins and the palomino snorted then was quiet.

Now the quarreling ceased.

Carl Lee's ears perked up and he moved a few steps closer to the house where he stilled the horse in the shade of the southern pine tree.

It started again.

The voice of his father. The voice of his grandfather.

"He's coming home to Ponca City now!" Samuel, his father, shouted.

"No way," said Gray in a voice tough as pig iron. "He's in the middle of classes and in the middle of summer."

"I'm the daddy and what I say goes."

"I agree," said Gray after a long pause and in what seemed like a lighter tone of voice.

Carl Lee's stomach bounced. "How could Grandpa

agree with him?" he whispered to himself as he tied the horse to the porch.

He quickened his steps up the stairs. *Too soon. Too soon to go home.* Then Gray clarified what he meant. "I agree that what you say goes. And I'd like to remind you that what you *said* in May was that Carl Lee would spend the whole summer here in Golden Pasture."

When Carl Lee opened the screen door he saw his father, all six foot seven of him, swaying like a tall tree in a fierce wind. He saw his tree tall father bend over and take a drink from a bottle of cheap wine.

"Hi, Dad," Carl Lee said, but there was no joy in his voice. He was not glad to see Samuel Jefferson.

"I'm taking you home," said Samuel, who looked past him as he spoke, he never ever looked at Carl Lee when he was talking to him.

"I'm not going," Carl Lee said. "You can't even take your ownself home." He crossed his angry arms, his heart stampeded under his wet shirt.

Gray set the rocking chair in motion.

Samuel took another swig from the wine jug, draining it before setting it aside. Then he said, "Been swimming in Opal Lake. Thought you were supposed to be in school."

"I was," Carl Lee said, befuddled. Maybe his father did look at him. But how? Out of the corner of his eye? "Yeah," he said absently answering his own question.

"Yessir! Don't be getting grown and surly now, Mr. Big Britches. I'll make you wet those blue jeans sure enough. And it won't be from the water in Opal Lake."

"I got a fool for a father," Carl Lee said, unable to

bridle his tongue. He turned to go change his wet clothes.

"Don't you turn your back on me. Just like your mama! Don't you turn your back on me!"

Gray started to rise from his chair to intervene between father and son but before he could do anything to stop him Samuel hurled himself at Carl Lee, knocking him to the floor.

"I'll teach you!" Samuel snarled and swung at Carl Lee.

Carl Lee's head spun with pain. Angrily, he twisted away and jumped up swinging. A reflex. He knocked the staggering Samuel back down.

When he realized what he had done, shame swamped him. He wheeled.

"You will mind me as long as you're a son of mine!" Samuel hollered after Carl Lee as the boy ran from the room and down the hall.

Carl Lee bent over in his desk chair by the window holding his bruised head in his hands. His head felt as big as a horse's.

"Leave here, Mr. Sam. Right now," Carl Lee heard his grandfather saying.

"You're teaching this boy to disobey me?" said Samuel, swaying to his feet.

"No," said Gray. "But I bound you this, he's said he's not going and I second that decision. He's not going anywhere with you drunk!"

"The whole world's against me," Carl Lee heard Samuel whine. "I can't even have my own son to myself."

When Carl Lee came out of the bathroom, he saw his father, nursing a black eye, whirl and go stumbling out of the house and down the steps, weaving across the

58

yard and out into the field toward the No Trespassing sign.

"Most likely, he'll sleep out in the field and be gone by morning," Gray said in a sad voice.

"Why does he act like that?" Carl Lee asked, still upset.

Gray didn't answer him at once. A look of longing and sadness etched the lines deeper in his face. "Maybe he resents you coming out here, being with me. He always wanted you just for himself. Even from birth."

Gray finally sighed, "When will he learn we can't build a fence around our feelings or the people we love."

"Love?" said Carl Lee, irony mocking his voice.

Carl Lee brooded, maybe Samuel wouldn't be gone in the morning. Maybe Samuel would come back from the No Trespassing pasture to raise him out of his sleep before daybreak.

"Maybe in order to cool things down, I'll have to cut the summer short and go home to Ponca City." Then remembering last year and Gray's anguished phone call to Ponca City when he couldn't find Carl Lee in the fields that fateful afternoon that Samuel had forced him home early, Carl Lee recommitted himself. "No," he said, "this time I'm standing my ground."

After chores, Carl Lee didn't do much homework, he kept staring at the No Trespassing sign and hoping that his father would leave him in peace in Golden Pasture.

That night in his dream he hit his father so hard the pain woke him up. The moon beaming through his window showed him a fist swollen fat from hitting the iron rail of his bed. The oppressive heat and his aching hand kept him in a sweat. He tossed and turned on the firm mattress for what seemed like an eternity before falling back off into a deep sleep.

He didn't know how long the rooster had been crowing when he woke up.

Terror drove him as he hopped out of bed and ran out of his room, down the hallway through the living room and opened the front door to look out.

His father's car was gone.

THE APPALOOSA

NOW IT WAS SATURDAY AGAIN, A WEEK SINCE
the fight with his father.

As Carl Lee went about his daybreak chore of milking
the cows, the long shadows of morning lay softly against
the Oklahoma landscape. A subtle patchwork of shade
subdued the blackjack trees, keeping out the light until
later.

The birds broke the quiet stillness, a choir of them,
calling gently, sweetly enchanting the air with their
warbling.

The rooster faithful to the dawn shadows crowed
intermittently and strutted up and down in his chicken
coop. His red comb crown catching the first glint of the
Saturday morning sun.

The patient nesting hens, fat with feathers and the
confidence that comes after laying an egg, spread out
their featherdresses proudly over their straw thrones and
clucked noisily.

When Saturday was half gone, Gray said, "Carl Lee,
I'm going into Boley. I'll be staying overnight. We're
celebrating Billingsley's birthday.

"Billingsley's gonna be seventy-two," he announced. "The old tribe of retired cowboys will be doing some serious partying this evening. In fact I intend to wear myself out. I'll be too tired to do anything after it's over but sleep.

"And you know, Carl Lee, I don't celebrate and drive." He picked up a bottle of his personally prepared loganberry wine that he aged especially for parties.

"So," Gray promised, "I'll spend the night and be back first thing in the morning. Before the dew dries in the northwest pasture, I'll be home."

"Don't worry about me," Carl Lee said. "Have yourself a good time, Grandpa."

As evening fell, Gray prepared to leave.

"Hey, special pony, how do I look?" Gray said. He was dressed in a straw hat, a long sleeve shirt, a leather beaded necklace peeping through his collar opening and a pair of cowboy britches. His boots had been polished until they gleamed.

As old as he is, my grandpa's still handsome, Carl Lee realized with a shock.

"You'll pass, mighty handsome for an old mule," he teased good-naturedly.

Gray grinned.

The steady rumbling of his grandfather's old truck starting up was a lonely sound.

It was strange being at the ranch without Gray.

The cows mooed to let Carl Lee know he wasn't completely alone.

And the five horses in the stable whinnied as though saying good-bye to Gray.

Carl Lee couldn't think about horses without thinking about his grandfather. Gray had taught him to ride the summer Carl Lee was five years old.

That summer Gray had placed him on the gentlest pony for that first riding lesson. Carl Lee was so proud he rode until the June bugs came out and then fell asleep in the saddle.

Carl Lee also remembered that later on that summer, the first week of September was the occasion of his first trip to the rodeo in Boley.

That Labor Day they had put the five horses in the horse trailer and hooked the trailer to the pickup. Carl Lee couldn't get over how well-mannered the horses were. Standing in the trailer quiet as shadows. In fact, their quietness on the long road to the rodeo was as amazing to him as the fact that horses sleep standing up. Perhaps they too were full of anticipation. The rodeo. A place where any horse could strut his stuff. Every since he had been five years old, his steady dream was to perform in the Boley Rodeo.

Carl Lee had learned how to run fast by watching the horses.

"How'd you learn to run like a horse?" his grandfather had asked him.

"I think like a horse," the five-year-old Carl Lee had responded.

"How's that?" asked Gray, the answer stopping him in his tracks.

"Four," answered Carl Lee. "I think I have four legs instead of two."

And he had demonstrated for his grandfather. Racing from the barn to the house.

Scratching his head, Gray said, "Twice as many legs, I guess that multiplies your speed all right."

And Gray had told everybody he knew, "My grandson really owns four legs instead of two, you just can't see the other pair."

He had a lot to be thankful to his grandfather for, Carl Lee thought as he went into the kitchen.

After warming up and eating some of Gray's hearty stew of potatoes, beef, onions and peas and the skillet bread that went with it, Carl Lee washed up the dishes.

He reached in the refrigerator and took out the slice of stone mountain watermelon, placed it on a saucer, sprinkled salt on it and settled down in his grandfather's rocking chair. The melon tasted red ripe and juicy sweet.

After he finished his dessert, he washed the saucer and his hands.

He went and got his Bible and started scripture searching in preparation for leading a discussion in Sunday School the next Sunday.

He started at Genesis and had been through the entire Bible when he came upon the first chapter of Revelation. He stopped at the third verse because it sounded like something his grandfather would say, "Blessed is he that readeth."

"Shoot," he said, putting the Bible down. "I wish Grandpa would come on home tonight."

Then he chastised himself for being selfish. Didn't his grandfather devote every summer to him? Surely, he could allow him one night out with his friend Billingsley without having Mrs. Nervalene Robinson come a mile down the road to stay with him. He was too old for Nervalene Robinson to baby-sit him on Billingsley's birthday as she had done in years past, and while she was there making dumplings or cornbread dressing or some other dish Gray didn't have in his corral of recipes.

"Maybe I'll watch a little tv," Carl Lee said to himself. He got up and turned on the tv.

There was one of those game programs with dollar bills flying through the air, lots of audience applause and contestants hopping up and down with joy, carbon copy giggles in their voices every time they got a correct answer. On other nights that he had watched he was entertained by their happy shenanigans, but tonight they just looked like somebody had wound them up.

He turned the dial again.

An old-fashioned movie. An ancient cowboy rode into a ghost town on his palomino horse and as he dismounted and tied his horse to the railing along the board sidewalks, he talked slow to the sheriff.

The old cowboy made Carl Lee think about his grandfather and how lonesome he was although Gray hadn't been gone a good two hours.

He turned the channel again.

A scary Alfred Hitchcock movie. He loved Alfred Hitchcock movies, but not tonight. He turned the dial again.

Nothing satisfied him. He flicked the switch to off.

He was restless. And even rocking in the rocking chair pretending he was his own grandfather didn't soothe him. He kept getting up and looking out the window.

The day was leaving. The sun falling over the horizon.

The ranch sounded strange and quiet. Even the cows had stopped mooing. And the five horses must have been standing up, asleep in their stalls.

Now what?

He could review his homework. He went to his room and picked up that poetry book.

He opened the book. Then he closed it.

No, he wasn't in the mood for memorizing that poem.

He looked out of the window.

A full moon stared him straight in the face when he studied the sky.

And the blackjack tree outside in the yard squatted in its own shadow.

The moon's reflection shone down and made the green alfalfa fields look scary. The fields glowed like phosphorus.

Everything added to his loneliness.

Then he realized much of the happiness around the ranch had a lot to do with his grandfather's presence. It was not just the old brick house, the fields and the trees, the cows or the white-washed barn that he enjoyed. Why, the sound of Gray's voice at night was like a light turned on in the dark.

Yet, as he thought about it he realized, it was more than the baritone bass of Gray's voice even.

He pictured the fast-slow movement of Gray's hands when he was frying skillet-hotwater cornbread. Something as simple as that. It made home, home.

He heard something cornered howl far away. And he shivered.

An owl flew past his window. Like a winged cloak in the dark.

Get a hold of yourself, he said.

Then there came the most eerie scream. The sound of crying, distress, but it was not a human voice.

It sounds like it's coming from. . . .

Yes, it was coming from the direction of the No Trespassing sign.

An animal was hurt.

But what animal?

Something cornered? Some dangerous thing he had never seen before?

There was danger in the woods.

Some wild bobcat at his throat?

A rattlesnake striking thigh-high above his boots on a dark night was a danger.

But he had been on coon hunts before at night. And it was pitch black when they hunted possums. Surely he wasn't afraid of any old rattlesnake.

But Gray had been with him those times. This was different.

No it wasn't a cornered animal, he thought, listening closer.

But what was it?

He was rooted to his chair.

Then the eerie cry again.

He gripped the chair's arms. If Gray was here, he'd know what to do. The two of them would put on their boots, grab their shotguns and ride over to see what was the matter.

But Gray was gone, over in Boley, dressed up, partying.

And he was here, a boy of twelve, alone with things hollering in the night.

The sound inched under his hairline and stuck there. Lay desperate in his ear.

Oh, the wailing.

The cry of hurt.

He couldn't sit still.

Soon he was up walking the floor.

The call of pain. He had to help.

He decided he wouldn't take the palomino. He would run over to that No Trespassing place and see what that was.

After all, he could run almost as fast as his horse.

He pulled on his boots.

The call came again, higher and more eerie.

He went into his bedroom and took his shotgun off the wall.

"This will never do, I can't run fast with this old gun," he said out loud.

He hung his gun back on the wall and hurried out the bedroom door.

He ran through the kitchen. Whatever was hurt, he was going to help. He couldn't take much more of that strange screaming.

Out the back door he flew, over the alfalfa phosphorous green fields, out past the alfalfa into a patch of wild indigo and wild sunflowers around a blooming redbud tree, over the planks bridging Opal Lake, running with the frog and cricket sound in his throat too, and through a copse of blackjack trees.

He ran on and on to the sound of the wavering, haunting cry.

He ran until he wanted to cry out for breath.

He paused only to unlatch the gate with the No Trespassing sign on it and pass into another field.

He ran on toward the sound.

69

A big lonely southern pine blocked his path just as a huge horned owl with a span of wings as long as he was tall flapped in front of him.

"What?" hollered Carl Lee. Then the creature took off steering between a pair of oak trees and on out of sight.

Into the night the raw cry of pain flew and stuck in his ear again.

And he was running toward whatever was making that sound.

Then he was upon it.

The crying thing.

It sat in a meadow, edged with goldenrod. Next to the goldenrod he spotted yellow primroses and daisies, all yellow and proud.

In a field already blooming in golden alfalfa flowers as though a special sun shone on this alfalfa field, a sun that did not beam any place else, he saw the most beautiful creature his eyes had ever beheld.

"An Appaloosa!" Carl Lee gasped. He was brown all over except on his back and on his hooves. "A raindrop horse," he whispered, noticing the white area on the loins and hips, the patterning of round spots like clouds.

The horse lay crying in the middle of this golden meadow, crying the most eerie cry.

What was wrong?

He ran to the horse and examined his legs. No leg was broken. And then he saw the nearby hole in the meadow.

He looked at the horse's black and white striped back hoofs.

Right away, he knew what had happened; the horse's

right back foot had stepped into the hole and he had strained a muscle trying to pull it out.

The Appaloosa had gotten down and couldn't get back up.

He would have to help the horse up. Take him to the barn near the house, put him in the stable and take care of him.

But he had no harness, no bridle.

He spied a honeysuckle vine running along the nearby fence.

He ran to the honeysuckle, pulled out a long piece of vine and made a wreath to put around the horse's neck.

The vine made excellent twine and he let one long piece of honeysuckle rope trail down from the wreath. And this became the bridle.

He soothed the horse, talked to him, coaxed him with a firm but gentle voice as he pushed, helping the horse rise.

Still crying the horse pulled himself up and followed Carl Lee without resisting him, led by the bridle of honeysuckle.

The Appaloosa walked along behind him dragging that hind leg.

Past the oak trees, the southern pine and on through the unlatched gate, past the copse of blackjack trees, across Opal Lake, and the redbud tree in blossom, the limping horse followed Carl Lee until the ranch house came into sight. They passed the house and went straight to the barn.

He knew what to do for a pulled muscle. Hadn't he seen his grandfather take care of horses before?

Pulling a muscle was one of the most painful accidents

to happen to a horse, next to having a broken leg.

Knowing this, Carl Lee continued to talk gently to the horse as he led him into the barn. The other horses neighed and seemed to look on from their stalls with compassionate eyes as Carl Lee helped the Appaloosa.

He knew the treatment for a pulled muscle.

The thing to do was to walk the horse awhile. He had already done that, bringing him from the golden pasture.

The other part of the remedy was to put heat on the muscle of the injured hind leg.

Although it was well past his bedtime by now, he stayed up tending the Appaloosa with liniment heat packs, whispering encouragement in his long ears.

Between applying the aromatic heat packs, he laid straw in an empty stable. Spread it around until it was even. The stable now was ready for the Appaloosa.

Soon the horse stopped crying.

Then Carl Lee led the horse to the straw stable. He didn't want to leave the Appaloosa in case he started crying with pain again and had to have the liniment packs applied again, so Carl Lee curled up alongside him in the straw and fell asleep.

He woke up from a deep sleep when he heard a rooster crowing.

And another sound.

The sound of his grandfather calling him.

"Carl Lee! Carl Lee!"

Carl Lee had a time orienting himself. Where was he? Not in his bed. He smelled straw, the sweat of horses, and the intense fragrance of honeysuckle.

It took him a little while to realize he was in the

stables. With the horses! With The Horse! The Appaloosa!

Wait until his grandfather heard!

He didn't holler back at his grandfather. He didn't want to startle the Appaloosa. He patted the raindrop horse and left the stall, securing it behind him.

He ran out of the barn into the growing sunlight.

"Here, here I am, Grandpa!"

"I went to your room. Your bed hadn't been slept in," Gray said worriedly.

"That's because I wasn't in it. I slept in the barn."

"What?"

Carl Lee told him all that had happened. And about the beautiful horse.

Gray stood there, stunned into silence.

"You mean the Appaloosa?" Gray asked when he found his tongue.

"Yes, that one." It was then Carl Lee realized he might be in trouble for going into the forbidden area, but he had thought only of an animal, out there hurt and alone. Now what would his grandfather do? His voice lumped in his throat and he shut up.

"I don't know about this," Gray said shaking his head after what seemed to Carl Lee like a century.

"Now let's go see him," his grandfather said.

They walked inside the barn.

Carl Lee brought some hay over to the horse and fed him.

Gray stood there still looking amazed at the way the wild horse responded to his grandson.

After a while he just shook his head, not saying much.

"Grandpa, can I keep him? Can he be my horse?"

"I don't know, son. He's wild. He needs to be out in the open pastures, with a bigger fence than we have for the rest of the horses. That's why he had his own acres over there. It took forever, but I fenced him in."

"Please, Grandpa. . . . Oh, please, I think I'll die if I can't have him."

"Well, no you won't. But we'll see."

Gray was trying to figure something out. But Carl Lee was so excited he couldn't pay much attention to his grandfather. The Appaloosa! The wonderful Appaloosa! He couldn't stand it.

" 'We'll see,' oh Grandpa!"

"That's enough for now," Gray said with sternness in his voice.

Then he continued, "Obviously the horse likes you. Maybe because you helped him when he was in pain. . . ." He scratched his gray head. "But I wouldn't try to ride him. He's bucked and busted more men than. . . ."

"What?" asked Carl Lee.

"I said I wouldn't try to ride him."

"He can't be ridden, Grandpa, he's got a pulled muscle."

"We'll see. We'll see," Gray kept saying, as they headed to the house.

In the kitchen Carl Lee peeled potatoes for breakfast and after they had sizzled crisp in the big black skillet, they sat down to a meal of old-fashioned hashbrowns with onions, scrambled eggs, buckwheat flapjacks and Alaga syrup, orange juice and broomwheat tea so strong you couldn't see the bottom of the cup.

Gray finally said, "Why you're just like your daddy in a way. He was crazy about horses too. Except that boy always did have fits."

"My daddy a boy?" said Carl Lee.

"Even I was a boy once upon a time," Gray said with amusement. "Your daddy had these crazy spells. Crazy about horses like I said. You got that from him naturally. That's for sure! It was a horse that made Samuel show his mettle. I thought I had Samuel figured out as the laziest, most no count teenager that ever passed through adolescence. As he got older he only got worse. But now I think maybe I was wrong for thinking that way."

"Grandpa? You wrong?"

Gray took a sip from his cup of broomwheat tea. Then he added remembering some old incident, "And Samuel was right. Once, your daddy loved a horse. I should've let him keep the horse after we caught him, but I wanted to show him off in that darn rodeo. He was a king, that horse."

"What horse? What are you talking about? What happened?" Carl Lee asked, sopping the last morsel of flapjack into the Alaga syrup.

"Oh, the horse became part of the rodeo. . . . And. . . . Never mind the in-between part," he said, cutting the story short noticing Carl Lee's ready feet pointing toward the back door. His bottom on the edge of the chair itching to leap up and run see about the Appaloosa.

"The upshot is Samuel and I never saw eye to eye about that incident. The horse ended up not his and not the rodeo's. But not free either. To a horse like that

75

freedom means being wild. That's something Samuel understands."

Gray emptied the last of the broomwheat tea from his cup. "Your daddy was wild. Samuel, Samuel, running wild, wild as any horse that bucked, stomped, and escaped the roundup in the New Mexico mountains out yonder. Staying out late, drinking rot gut and tanglefeet wine. Chasing women like a stallion chasing mares. The only time he got his mind together was when that horse appeared. I've never seen one man make over a horse the way Samuel did over that long ago stallion. And the horse liked him. Wouldn't let any other rider come near him except Samuel.

"Samuel didn't want that horse in the rodeo though. Said it was a shame and a disgrace for the horse to be in the same arena as some of those peasant ponies and nobody nags."

Although Carl Lee was interested in hearing about his father's teenaged years, he thought he heard the Appaloosa bleat with pain. He scrambled out the back door, forgetting about washing the dishes and taking out the garbage, barely hearing Gray's last words.

"Your daddy's never forgiven me. Never. Never. Never forgiven me for the horse named Thunderfoot."

CLOUDY

THE SUNDAY MORNING CRICKETS CONTIN-
ued their soft June calls, vibrating as Gray milked the
cows and Carl Lee groomed and brushed the horses. The
cricket sound of peace and summer and all that's right
with the world lay over the ranch like a net. Through
the holes in the net Carl Lee heard the chee-chee birds,
the mockingbirds and starlings and meadow larks.

Chores over, breakfast finished, they bathed in preparation for church.

Now they were in Gray's sparsely furnished bedroom
getting dressed.

"Can't I stay home just this one Sunday?" Carl Lee
begged as he ironed the white shirts they were to wear.

"No, partner, we have social commitments too, you
know," said Gray, his thick fingers searching his box of
cuff links. He selected two twist-shaped cuff links, a pair
of silver lassos.

Carl Lee knew by Gray's tone there was no talking
his grandfather out of going to church.

"I'd never hear the end of it. Next thing we know all

those nosy women in the church would be arriving with baskets of food, snooping and sniffing around, claiming I need another wife."

No getting out of it then. They were definitely getting ready to attend the Golden Pasture African Methodist Episcopal Church.

He finished laying out the clothes on his grandfather's bed.

His grandfather's iron bed still had the last quilt his dead wife had patched on top. The quilt served both as a decorative spread in summer and as warmth in the winter.

Otherwise, it was a man's room. But one that was orderly. Shoes and boots lined up in the closet. Shirts and ties on one side. Cowboy clothes, coveralls and overalls hanging on the other.

Gray handed Carl Lee a pair of cuff links in the shape of spurs and they finished getting dressed.

"Here we are harnessing ourselves in these contraptions just like any other horse or mule," said Gray, standing in front of his bedroom mirror. With a grimace he perfected a knot in his navy blue tie.

"Let's see, my young stallion," he added, checking to see if Carl Lee's light blue tie was straight.

It was, but he gave it an extra twist anyway.

"Well, we're early as usual."

Gray picked up his old King James Bible and Carl Lee went to his room and fetched his newer Bible. They headed for the truck.

"I sure do wish I could spend the day with my horse," said Carl Lee, as they roared across Opal Lake's bridge.

"I know how you feel," said Gray.

"Can I name him?"

"Name him?" echoed Gray. "What would you call him?"

Carl Lee was quiet for a moment remembering the first time he saw the Appaloosa. The raindrop horse. He recalled how the brown horse looked with the splashes of silver on his withers and the black spots dappling his loins and hips like storm clouds on a moonlit canvas.

"I think I'll call him Cloudy."

"Cloudy?" said his grandfather, amazement in his voice. After a while he said slowly, "I like that."

"Cloudy," said Carl Lee.

Soon they were rolling into Golden Pasture. They stopped in the middle of Main Street and then parked in front of the white wooden church. They walked up the red brick steps leading to the entrance.

Once inside they pulled off their hats and walked down the aisle.

The congregation was singing "Bringing in the Sheaves," and Jessie and Norman scooted over so Carl Lee could sit next to them in the pew occupied by the younger people.

Gray went farther to the front and sat next to his old friend, Billingsley, a bald-headed man as tall and muscular as Carl Lee's grandfather.

Billingsley's head looked like a full moon shining in the middle of the day.

Carl Lee mischievously wondered if Billingsley shined his head when he finished shining his boots.

He felt a drake's feather tickle his insides at the thought of Billingsley busy shining his head, making the rag pop as he polished his scalp until it sparkled.

He was so full of excitement about the horse that seeing Billingsley's bald head gave him a kind of emotional release. He wanted to laugh so bad his stomach hurt holding it in.

"What's so funny?" whispered Jessie, noticing Carl Lee's belly jiggling up and down.

"What's up?" echoed Norman.

Once he got over being tickled about Billingsley's head, he thought the two old friends looked dignified and as if they knew everything important there was to know in the world.

Too, he wondered how he would look when he got that age, if his head would be bald like Billingsley's or with hair full and white like his grandfather's. And however it looked, he wondered if his head would have as much sense in it as theirs.

Now he threw himself wholeheartedly into the singing, "We shall all rejoice when bringing in the sheaves."

His voice was almost deep, not quite. He was presently a tenor on his way to being a bass. As he sang, he remembered what his grandfather told him, "Put some authority in your voice when you make music, but color it sweet."

The notes of the song flew to and from the pews of women whose perfume drifted like flowers in the air. The sweet rhythm rained over the younger girls sitting next to their mothers, their ribbons on their heads like colorful streamers.

And the voices floated along his own row among the congregation of boys in white shirts and ties, just like him, but no coats. Boots shined. Short hair, some cut the old-fashioned way, by setting a bowl on the boy's head and cutting around it. But all the short hairstyles boasted neat parts and were brushed back until each hair lay in its own pasture.

After the song ended, Reverend Honeywell preached a sermon about the four horses in Revelations.

"Revelations, sixth chapter; fifth and sixth verses. 'And when he had opened the third seal, I heard, Come and see. And I beheld, and lo a black horse; and he that sat on him had a pair of balances in his hand. . .'" But Carl Lee's mind was on his own horse, and so he didn't pay much attention to the minister's sermon.

Before he knew it Reverend Honeywell was saying the benediction, "May the Lord watch between me and thee while we are absent one from another. Until we meet again, let the church say Amen."

"Amen," the congregation sighed.

Carl Lee walked out of the church and into the light and onto the red brick church steps with the rest of the congregation. He spoke politely to everybody, but he didn't want to linger very long. And his eyes kept making silent pleas every time he could catch Gray's glance.

After only a few minutes of standing on the green lawn with Norman and Jessie watching the ribbon-haired girls and calling them delicious names like "Golden Cookies," "Nutmeg Honeys," and "Sweet Chocolate Drops," Carl Lee was ready to go.

Gray, sensing Carl Lee's anxiety, talked only a few minutes to the widow women.

"Oh, Gray, your grandson's going to be as tall as you are, I declare!" said Nervalene Robinson, the mother of the church who used to baby-sit Carl Lee when he was younger. Now she was somewhere in her nineties, peering at Carl Lee through her bifocals.

"Yes, the boy's amazing. A pedigree. Why, he sprints as fast as a race horse. He's as surefooted as a quarter horse. Got the hindquarters of a Lipizzan, runs as smooth as a Morgan and is as handsome as a Clydesdale." Gray stuck out his chest.

As anxious as he was to return home, Carl Lee smiled in spite of himself. He didn't know what to think of his grandfather's comparing him to horses, but he liked it.

On the other hand he knew his grandfather's comparisons could be cutting too. When Nervalene Robinson asked him, "And how's that son of yours in Ponca City doing?" his grandfather didn't bite his tongue but looked Mrs. Robinson straight in the eye and said, "Still cutting up. A wild ass on the loose."

When the astonished Nervalene Robinson, leaning on her cane, looked at him with her mouth open, he said, "It's in the Bible. A wild ass on the loose. Hosea, eighth chapter; ninth verse."

At that, Nervalene Robinson gave a relieved little laugh. His grandfather said good day then turned and said a few words to Billingsley, but they didn't talk long either.

Finally, Gray was saying his farewells and heading straight for the blue pickup, his Bible tucked under his arm.

As they motored down the road toward home, Carl Lee sat on the edge of his seat. Way after while they were passing over Opal Lake's bridge. He barely heard the frogs crowing and the crickets fussing at the heat.

And the sound of the drakes quacking in a chorus was muted. Once the red brick house came into view, he let out a great sigh.

Gray had barely parked when Carl Lee busted out of the pickup and ran straight to the barn. Cloudy was up and moving around, but he still limped a little.

Carl Lee cleaned out the Appaloosa's stall and strewed new straw.

He walked the horse a bit.

Then he applied more liniment cloths.

"Pretty soon, he won't need those hot packs anymore," said Gray, leaning over feeling the horse's leg.

"He's healing fast all right," Carl Lee agreed.

"I bet in one week, you'll hardly know he pulled this muscle," said Gray.

"He's gorgeous," said Carl Lee. "The most handsome horse I've ever seen."

"He's a magic horse all right."

"Magic?" said Carl Lee, lifting his eyes from packing the liniment cloth to the horse's withers. All right then, he decided, a handsome magic horse. That was Cloudy to the tee.

"Hey, mustang, don't you think you ought to take off your church clothes?"

Carl Lee, in his excitement, had forgotten all about that. He ran into the house and changed.

A week passed and Cloudy had lost his limp.

Carl Lee found a halter and a bridle in the barn and put them around the horse's neck. Then he walked him all around the barn and across the alfalfa field, but he stayed away from the No Trespassing area.

Gray was yelling something.

"What?" Carl Lee yelled back.

"Yes," Carl Lee answered, "he let me put the halter on him."

From where he stood in the fields he could see Gray hitch up his britches then scratch his head in wonder and yell something about "You're your daddy's son, all right."

At the end of the next week, Carl Lee experienced the spirit of Cloudy.

Every time he tried to mount him, the horse tossed his mane, shook his neck violently in warning and gave a belligerent snort.

After much coaxing, Carl Lee finally mounted the horse and rode him a short distance.

Again he saw Gray near the front steps yelling and waving his hat.

"What?" said Carl Lee.

"Yes," Carl Lee hollered back, "he let me mount him and ride him."

At last he saw his grandfather hunching his shoulders and shaking his gray head until Carl Lee thought it would roll right off his neck.

Later that day they put all six horses out in the pasture. Standing near the fence, now covered with wild raspberries and wild blackberries, the horses lounged in the shade of a redbud tree. Then they moseyed on down by the lake, flicking the biting flies from their backs and constantly whipping their long tails like motorized fly swatters.

Carl Lee and Gray brought two chairs out to the

pasture and sat under the tree watching the horses drink from nearby Opal Lake.

Carl Lee's hand flew up and rubbed a tickling burn on his neck. "Darn mosquito."

Gray said, "Mighty sneaky pest the mosquito."

"Sneaky?"

"The way he lands so light on you. Won't put his weight on you like a bee or a wasp. No. The mosquito lands so light you can't feel him, till he's through, that is. When he's sucked his fill of your blood, he takes off, singing his mosquito song. Reminds me of some people I know. Just as treacherous. You don't know you've been stung till they've done you in."

"Maybe they ought to have a repellent for those kind of folk," Carl Lee said.

His grandfather gave a belly laugh. "Insect repellent for people?"

"Why not?" said Carl Lee, letting his imagination run.

"I only heard of insect spray to keep off bugs. If they had insect spray for people, I'd buy up a store's worth," said Gray. "There are folks out there so sneaky they'll try and sell you a horse with no legs.

"But back to this insect spray to keep off bugs. We didn't have any spray in the old days. We used smoke and blackberry juice to keep the biting mosquitoes away. Still works today," he said reaching for a bunch of wild blackberries, squeezing them through his strong black hands until the juice ran down. Then he rubbed his skin until it stained even darker.

Carl Lee followed suit. The berries stained the skin around his fingers too, creating a new hue. He was a red clay boy with the juicy darkness of the berries blending in with his color.

Inevitably the conversation turned to horses. "If only I had the eyes of a horse," said Carl Lee. "If I could just look forward and backward at the same time, just like Cloudy. . . . "

"I like your eyes just as they are," said Gray.

"The horse pays well for that ability. Although one eye can look in front of him and the other can look behind him, he has a blind spot. Can't see what's right in front of his nose. Same thing with a jackass."

Then Gray went on to add, "Your daddy's got a mind like a jackass's eyes. He's still in mourning over losing too much. But he can't see you at all. The miracle standing right there in front of his eyes." A sadness claimed his face, and then all at once his old eyes brightened as though a hidden candle was lit in them. "But I remember one miracle he did work. One rodeo night."

"**I** HAVE TO TELL YOU ABOUT THE NIGHT your father worked a miracle. The night he saved a horse's life."

Carl Lee stared into his grandfather's eyes. The look and the sound of Gray's voice took Carl Lee back through time until he too was at the rodeo in Boley watching the events unfold.

"It was raining that night at the Boley Rodeo. The rain started at first in little sprinkles, just misting. The grandstand overflowed with folks from Maine to Mississippi from California to Kansas. And the star of the show was Thunderfoot. Thunderfoot was an Appaloosa that was captured wild, sold to the rodeo — and no man could break him."

"Where did he come from?" asked Carl Lee.

"Whoa boy! That's another story."

Gray continued.

"The horse was beginning to look haggard, to show the effect of being trotted around, mistreated from rodeo to rodeo. And this night a rider named Hellhound came to Boley expressly to ride Thunderfoot.

"The crowd ached for action, thirsted for a taste of Thunderfoot's blood.

"Earlier in the day Samuel heard Hellhound say to a wrinkled-faced cowboy in a broken-down hat, 'I'm going to break that horse tonight if I have to kill him.'

"The news flew like chee-chee birds, *Hellhound's gonna break that horse tonight if he has to kill him.*

"The message got around from barbecue pit to barbecue pit.

"Hellhound's boasting could have been the sauce the rodeo fans put on their ribs, his words stayed in their mouths and flavored the food and the atmosphere of the rodeo gathering.

"Now Hellhound was an ornery cuss. He would do anything to break a horse.

"Used his spurs like a butcher knife.

"Left horses bleeding and sometimes blinded.

"And he only rode once a year. It was always an occasion. He'd wait until a horse had built up a reputation for himself and then he'd appear.

"He was invincible, they say. But Samuel thought he was a coward.

"'We never should have sold this horse to the rodeo, Daddy,' Samuel said. 'You should've let me keep him!'

"Hellhound waited until a horse had been worn down by the other less skilled riders and then he would come along like some long lost hero out of the Oklahoma hills bragging, boasting about being the greatest bronc buster in these here parts.

"'Show me the animal I can't ride. I want to see him,' he ranted.

"An uneven match as far as Samuel was concerned.

"'Hellhound's more animal than any horse I ever met,' the teenaged Samuel said to me.

"Hellhound always wore yellow, perhaps to match his yellow eyes. The yellow was different, as if he had dipped his outfit in a special vat of dye whose color he borrowed from a yellow flame.

"That night he looked fairly incandescent.

"When he talked directly to Samuel or breathed in Samuel's face, Samuel had to turn away or move so Hellhound was standing downwind from him.

"'That's how he conquers wild horses,' Samuel whispered to me. 'Stuns them with his stinky breath.'

"'I am the baddest cowboy that ever crouched in a saddle!' Hellhound swore.

"Hellhound made fun of anybody a horse threw. 'Look at that baby, ought to be home still nursing his mama,' he said of a Guthrie man whose back got busted.

"The crowd had reached a frenzy of excitement. They always saved the most special event of the day until last, way past sundown.

"The clowns clowned more that night. People drank more, bringing their own red home brew, a fermentation of raisins, potatoes and anything else that'll mix with a pound of sugar and yeast. After they had run it off for two weeks, it was so strong it'd tear your head off.

"Half the folks in the stands were drunk from that red tanglefeet, so alcoholic and strong it'd tangle your feet and your mind.

"Then they did what the old-timers advised never to do, they split open stone mountain watermelons, the sweetest kind in Oklahoma, and mixed drink and melons.

A bad combination. In an atmosphere like that anything might happen.

"Not wanting to miss a thing, I stayed as sober as Reverend Millhouse over in the holiness church.

"The bulldoggers finished their bulldogging, the steer wrestlers finished wrestling their steer, and the bareback riders bucked and hopped off the backs of their horses in one piece either with no bones out of place or with backs broken.

"A storm threatened.

"Over the heads of the rodeo crowd angels roller-skated in the sky. The sound deafened the ordinary confusion.

"And the clouds whipped up a show that kept all their attention and their faces tilted up.

"Then the wind started.

"If the wind is the breath of God, He must have been having a coughing fit that night. Even the thick windows of the cars that get to the rodeo early and line the fences of the arena trembled and shook and the weather-beaten railings circling the arena rattled so hard they fell away like toothpicks.

"In the meantime all the horses, bulls and steers kicked the sides of their chutes with a banging noise, adding to the clamor.

"The loudspeaker clacked, filled with static. One old-timer said, 'I'm leaving this place,' as he picked up his gear, eyes on the sky. Samuel understood then why some folks won't turn on anything electrical when a storm's in the area. Old-fashioned folk turn off all the lights and sit quiet. Won't even answer the telephone. 'When God's working, I don't need to be busy,' the bowlegged cowboy said on his way out of the stands.

"There was something syncopated and dangerous in the air.

"That night was as different from regular night as daylight and darkness; dawn and dusk; midnight and morning. It was a night fit for the hounds of hell. It took night to its extreme. Who could rightly compare it to any other night they'd known?

"At first it was just drizzling, with the loud noises from up above.

"At the same time the loudspeaker announced, 'And now for the event of the evening, we have Hellhound riding Thunderfoot.'

"I was standing right next to Thunderfoot's chute with Samuel. As was Hellhound's habit, he was lollygagging around the grandstand so the people could see him. He always took his time about going to the chute.

"The rodeo fans leaned forward, a terrible quiet descended momentarily and hovered over the arena.

"Hellhound mounted Thunderfoot and the horse bucked and snapped, kicking up his heels, wild-eyed beyond his usual rage.

"The horse, feeling the devil on his back, whirled and bucked fiercely. Thunderfoot performed so spectacularly, he was getting the best of Hellhound who at this moment was hanging on for dear life.

"Hellhound, wall-eyed with worry, was intent on not being bested. He began pulling his dirty tricks, cutting the horse with his spurs. Blood flew like rain. And people commenced to crying, grown folk hugging their bottles of tanglefeet and just letting the tears fall unashamedly when they thought Thunderfoot was finally done for.

"Then the sky split open with white lightning, and a

sound like a giant horse, some mythical ancestral, granddaddy of all horses, stampeded from a cloud causing thunder so loud it distracted Hellhound. In that quick moment, Thunderfoot whipped Hellhound to the ground.

"In a halting gallop, Thunderfoot ran to the side of the arena where Samuel and I watched.

"On the other side of the arena, Hellhound picked himself up and started running after the horse, determined to get back on him and finish the job.

"That's when Samuel bolted into the arena, caught up with Thunderfoot and told the horse, 'I'll save you.'

"The Appaloosa, his coat slippery with blood, was so grateful he forgot to kick. His eyes streaked red with fire held the kind of terror that perhaps only a proud, untamed horse knows.

"But he obeyed Samuel.

"And that horse let the tender rider mount him.

"Thunderfoot and Samuel looked like two phantoms in the wind, under cover of a cloud. The rodeo fans couldn't tell who the rider was. But the horse, now he was obvious. Nobody moved like Thunderfoot.

"But Thunderfoot was so injured, he couldn't run as well as he used to and Hellhound was gaining on them.

"The crowd, up out of their seats, urged Thunderfoot and his rider to escape.

"'Go!' they hollered in one wave of sound, but some of the thunder had been bled out of Thunderfoot.

"Then just when it looked like Hellhound might catch Thunderfoot and his mystery rider, the fans decided to get in the act.

"Outraged, they stormed out of the stands and swooped down on the shameless Hellhound and collared him.

They couldn't let him hurt Thunderfoot anymore. The horse had thrown him fair and square. The horse had won. There in the pouring rain, the rodeo fans kicked and cursed Hellhound, perhaps for all the other proud horses he'd violently subdued with his spurs. They beat the Oklahoma stew out of him. That varmint. And left him in the middle of the arena with his yellow suit in tatters.

"Hellhound dragged himself up out of the mud and swore one day he'd get even.

"He never showed his face again in Boley or any other Oklahoma rodeo.

"It is said he went to the New Mexico mountains searching for Thunderfoot, sure whoever took him had freed him back to the mountains. They say today he roams the world still looking for the wild Appaloosa determined to finish the job he started."

Gray sighed, bringing Carl Lee back to the present and the smell of the alfalfa pasture and the sweat of the horses.

Carl Lee, thinking about Samuel saving Thunderfoot, was so excited, he couldn't breathe for a moment. "Grandpa!"

His own father a hero!

He looked toward the horses at his own Appaloosa. But Cloudy was grazing, so Carl Lee couldn't see his eyes, but he imagined Cloudy with that penetrating look in his brown eyes, a look that Carl Lee decided must be the way horses look when they smile.

THE LEGEND OF
THUNDERFOOT

AUGUST CAME GALLOPING IN LIKE A BAND OF horses.

There was only one more week of summer school left. Every chance he could get away from studying Carl Lee spent in the barn or in the pasture with Cloudy.

Today he was joined in the barn by Gray and Billingsley.

"Grandpa," said Carl Lee who was rubbing down Cloudy while the horse nibbled at the hay, "since I'm going to ride in the rodeo this year, I need as much information about it as I can get. I want Cloudy to be a star. How does he compare to Thunderfoot and some of those other famous horses I hear you and Mr. Billingsley talking about?"

"Going to the rodeo, yes," said Gray as he inspected the stables for cleanliness, "riding in it, now I don't know about that. We'll have to see how you do in school and what kind of show you're doing for us, right, Billingsley? You see, B.B., he's keeping his horse trick a secret, when are you going to let me in on it, Carl Lee?"

"Won't be long, Grandpa, I promise," said Carl Lee.

"Oh, go ahead, tell him about one of the rodeo stars. Tell him about Black Out," suggested Billingsley.

Gray shook his head.

"Then tell him about Broken Bones. Now there's a story."

"No," said Gray, inspecting the bottom of a stall, secretly pleased at the neat arrangement of clean hay spread out evenly.

When his inspection was done, he started to say no horse stories today, he was feeling tired, but looking at his grandson, standing there rubbing Cloudy, with that curious expression in his eyes, Gray had a change of heart.

"All right, then," he said, selecting a bale of hay and making it into a seat.

His older buddy and Carl Lee did likewise.

"I'll tell you about how we caught the greatest rodeo horse of them all — Thunderfoot.

"It was a cloudy day when we came across Thunderfoot. We had been running this pack of wild horses for a week. It was in the far mountains of New Mexico. These broncs were the hardest bunch we had ever run. And like I say it had been cloudy, cloudy. Storms and rivers of water pouring from the sky. I thought the horse I was riding was a fast horse, since I had caught him years ago and tamed him myself, but there was a horse in the bunch we were trying to catch who could run circles around mine. It was the darndest thing I ever saw.

"There we were wet to the skin, soaked on down to the bone. And we didn't have sense enough to stop. It was like we were being driven by forces outside our control. We were obsessed with catching this horse.

"It was hard to even get a look at him. He looked like a thunderbolt out of nowhere, a bolt from the blue, as transitory as smoke, a brown slash of earth cutting across the land, a fugitive on four legs. But that glimpse only served to pull us on, riding behind him. He took us over some rough, rough territory and some only God had seen. Landscapes I thought I dreamed, mesquite bushes, sagebrush, tumbleweed, mountains shaped by mist, so dense they looked purple until you got right up on them.

"And once I saw gushing water flowing out of a stone right on the rib of the mountain. That was about the time we lost the third person on our team." He was silent for a minute, as though paying his respects to the lost cowboy. Then he continued.

"They say in some of those places the earth just opens up and swallows a man and his horse. But that's an Indian legend more ancient than I am. Still we never saw Hopkins again. We searched a whole day for him, but to no avail. Then as was the unwritten law of cowboys in the wild, we went on with our pursuit.

"We chased that phantom of a horse, his mane flying out behind him, his court of horses bringing up the rear. Racing along almost as fast as he was, they had to be sure-footed to keep up with him.

"I bound you I saw in Thunderfoot's entourage one of every kind of horse in these parts.

"It looked like he had personally inspected every tribe of horses in the area and selected the fastest, sleekest, most magic thoroughbred out of each family to ride with him.

"I saw a palomino, an albino, a morgan and a mustang, but he led them all — this raindrop horse, this Appaloosa — this Thunderfoot.

"I tell you, he was a legend. Once when we stopped only for a moment, we saw him standing on a ledge, standing far off looking at us as if to mock us for our tiredness.

"We had stopped to eat, but when I saw that beauty staring down at us from his high ledge, I told Billingsley, come on! And we left food, plate and all and mounted our horses and started off again.

"Before we could blink an eye Thunderfoot had disappeared from the cliff. Everything about that day was fleeting, as transient as the clouds.

"Sometimes the wind would blow the clouds and the storm would move. But the horse was following the clouds.

"When we'd lose sight of him all we'd have to do is look up in the sky and see where the darkest cloud was and that's when we'd get sight of him again.

"Then off we'd go, dashing through the red mud, the hoofs of the horses ahead pounding the ground, making their own kind of distant thunder.

"Six days later, we were still chasing. The folks at home told us later they thought we had fallen off a canyon and become food for the buzzards or that we had toppled into one of those holes the Indians tell us separate this world from the one below.

"We were lucky, only one of us had disappeared. We weren't quitters; we raced on. That horse was in our blood by then.

"It was get him or die out there in the New Mexico

mountains, struck down by lightning or sliding through the slippery mud off into a canyon.

"And we had to have him.

"We didn't stop for anything. We ate from the saddle. Hardtack and biscuits and hurried sips of water from our canteens.

"It was often dark when we passed under thick brush there through the New Mexico mountains, following the storm as we were. Things took on shadows and shapes they did not ordinarily have.

"I'm not sure why the horse headed for the makeshift corral we had made in that canyon.

"He started directly for the wedge.

"Maybe he was still following that cloud.

"I know he was too smart to be hedged in. The cloud was so low, it looked like the horse was descending from it.

"I don't know. Maybe there was something wrong in the sky. He didn't seem tired. He made an error.

"He turned down the cliff, following the cloud, headed for the canyon, shrieking. The most unearthly, lacerating bellow.

"Then that awful echo: the wild band of horses, answering him.

"Pretty soon, he was at a point where he couldn't turn around.

"We had him.

"They were hemmed in.

"I can still hear the raw horse sound of anguish today. The horse hollered in a voice that was almost human.

"Round and round he stamped. Trapped. For the first time in his life."

Gray paused, changed positions on his seat of hay. "We brought him back to the rodeo at Okmulgee. They couldn't tame him there.

"Then what happened to him, happened to many wild horses that wouldn't be broken: He was sent around on the circuit from show to show. He became the highlight of every rodeo from Okmulgee to Muskogee. Thunderfoot, the horse that wouldn't be broken. The horse that broke the riders. The horse that gave the ambulances a reason for lining up.

"In spite of his haughty anger and wildfire temper and the violence he heaped on any rider crazy enough to mount him, Thunderfoot was loved by many.

"They had horse dolls carved in his likeness. Horse blankets with his image on them. Pennants and flags featured Thunderfoot, that mane stretched out, the way I remembered him when we captured him. A free raindrop of a horse descending out of a cloud."

Gray paused, then continued.

"It's a sad thing, the love-hate relationship the rodeo public has with horses that won't be broken. Most of them were ridden until they were crippled, or otherwise injured and then there was only one thing to do. Shoot to kill."

Gray shook his head.

"A bitter end. They send dead horses to the meat packer. After the butcher gets through. . . . Think about it. Something beautiful you found in a canyon, running free, ending up on somebody's kitchen shelf in a tin can labeled dog food. Life's a riddle.

"But Thunderfoot was lucky. Samuel stole him before he wound up dead. He was one of the ones who would

101

never be tamed, at least not that way, although people kept hoping he would and wouldn't be, rodeo after rodeo. They took him from town to town, but he still wouldn't be ridden. It would take a miracle to tame him. But like I said, Samuel took him."

"And Samuel, my own father, stood up to Hellhound," said Carl Lee.

"Hellhound never knew who did it, but he vowed to kill the horse and the man next time he came across them."

Gray went on, "Samuel loved that horse. Maybe he recognized something of himself in Thunderfoot. Some free spirit that hated taming."

"You say he stole him, what if the rodeo committee knew? . . . " asked Carl Lee.

Gray explained, "The rodeo committee had a special meeting and decided the horse had had enough. They said whoever took him was justified."

"What happened to Thunderfoot? Where did he go?"

"That's something your father may tell you one day."

After saying that, Gray got up off his bale of hay and walked slowly toward the house, deep in memory. His friend Billingsley silently stepped beside him.

Carl Lee rubbed Cloudy's mane and thought about Thunderfoot. A horse made tame.

FEAR

CARL LEE AND HIS FRIENDS, NORMAN AND Jessie, sat cooling their boots on one of their favorite after-school spots, a stretch of fence nestled in the low valley, surrounded by the low hills of Gray's ranch. Behind their horses tethered to the posts, the golden alfalfa fields bloomed.

Honeysuckle spiced the air. Yellow blossoms stuck up their gay heads in the wild dandelions too.

"I was afraid I wasn't going to make it," said Carl Lee.

"Well, looks like you did, and with flying colors too. I thought Miss Monroe's teeth were going to fly out of her face, she was grinning, showing all thirty-twos so hard when you recited that poem. Show off!" Jessie accused.

"Oh, get up off him," said Norman. "You weren't too bad yourself reciting that poem. 'Listen to that enunciation,' Miss Monroe said, eyes lit up like two candles, her smile so bright the whole classroom almost got blinded. You didn't miss a word, you even paused at the commas. You both make me sick!"

"We might make you sick, but I don't see you crying," Carl Lee grinned. "Let me see that report card," he demanded.

Norman was up and off running. Plump as he was, he had some speed. He gave them quite a chase. But Carl Lee caught him and held him while Jessie took the card out of his pocket and looked at it.

"An A!" Jessie whistled.

"Yeah, in Miss Monroe's class, but check out the C in math," said Norman, sprawled on the alfalfa, out of breath from running so hard.

They counted their winning grades and their so-so marks, nobody had anything to be ashamed about.

After they finished horsing around, they crawled back up on the fence.

"We didn't have anything to be afraid of after all, did we?" asked Carl Lee.

"Yeah, but fear comes anyway," said Norman. "I'm afraid I'll be five feet all my life, even though I know I'll grow some more."

"Fear's like that all right."

"I'm afraid my daddy will die," said Norman.

"That my mama will," said Jessie

"That my grandfather will throw me off the ranch," said Carl Lee.

"That one day the world will blow up before I can get to see it."

"That no girl will ever want me."

"That some girl will!"

"That my daddy will say I can't ride in the rodeo," said Carl Lee.

"He wouldn't do that," said Jessie. "Would he?"

"Anyway, how would he know you were going to ride?"

"My grandfather wrote him a letter and told him I might ride this year," said Carl Lee.

Nobody knew what to say about that, they could only wait and see.

"How will you know what he'll say?"

"Oh, he'll write and let us know." Carl Lee shivered. Every letter he'd taken out of the mailbox from his father had been a threat. He didn't know what would be worse, receiving a letter before the rodeo or not receiving anything at all so he could just hope his father wouldn't respond, meaning he didn't care one way or the other.

They all thought about this awhile, then Jessie went on to discuss fears in general. "I'm afraid I'll do something awful and embarrass myself to death."

"I wonder what girls are afraid of," Carl Lee said.

"Now that Mary Jane Morgan couldn't ever be afraid of failing anything, as smart as she is, could she?"

They discussed this for a while.

After they had exhausted what each girl looked like in the class and who they thought was the prettiest and the smartest, they ended up talking about horses.

"What is it that horses don't do ordinarily?" Carl Lee asked Norman and Jessie.

"Well they don't talk," Norman said, scooting his hat farther up off his brow.

"They don't play the piano or the flute," said Jessie.

"That's not what I mean. What spooks a horse?" said Carl Lee.

Just then he saw the ugly hobo he'd noticed just last week slither past them down the road.

"Who is that man?"

"Looks like a creature from the deep," said Norman.

"He's got yellow fox eyes." Carl Lee felt spiders walking up his neck. Where the man's feet walked, Carl Lee imagined he saw fox tracks. He hopped off the fence and mounted his horse. "Guess I'd better be moseying along," he said uneasily, still eyeing the man as he slinked out of sight. The talk of fear had spooked them all.

Still, he hurried his horse home, not bothering to stop and wade at Opal Lake. Not bothering to check the mailbox with its red flag lifted. He hurried past the cows mooing in the pasture.

"God, it's hot! Alfalfa smells so hot it's almost cooking! Like . . . fire!"

He sniffed. An acrid stench smothered the air and by the time he approached the hill leading down to the ranch house, he saw a curl of smoke coming from the direction of the barn where the alfalfa hay was stored.

The barn. The horses!

"Cloudy!"

By now he heard the horses shrieking.

"Fire! Fire!" he called.

His grandpa ran to the porch, looked at Carl Lee hightailing the palomino to the smoking barn and hollered on his way back in the house. "Stay back, Carl Lee. I'm calling the fire department!"

Carl Lee knew he was supposed to stay away from the barn fire, but he couldn't help himself. The bales of hay exploded like firecrackers and the dark smoke billowed in pluming clouds.

He leaped off the palomino and ran to the barn.

He pushed open the door, and he knew somehow that the scarecrow bum had started this, but how? Trespassing, napping in the hay, falling asleep with a cigarette in his sagging mouth, a cigarette whose ashes sparked the fire.

"Coward of a bum!" Why hadn't the bum called for help or at least saved the horses while there was time.

Carl Lee put his arm over his forehead and tried to peer through the thick smoke.

His eyes stung.

Every time he took a breath, he coughed.

The horses shrieked, tossed their manes and stamped around in a tight circle.

Any second and they would stampede and kill each other, but they would not pass through the fire, even though there was a narrow passageway they could make it through to safety.

"Come on! Come on!" Carl Lee hollered.

But the horses only screamed louder.

Through the dense smoke, and the terrible pop of hay bales exploding, he could make out Cloudy.

He ran over to him, trying to remember what he had heard Gray say a long time ago, that's right, a horse's greatest fear is fire. His grandfather had told him, "A horse won't ever cross a path of fire."

What to do?

The pathway to safety was narrowing every second.

He leaped on Cloudy's back and covered the horse's

eyes with his hands. Then dug his heels in Cloudy's side.

"Go, boy!"

And Cloudy, through a great act of trust, moved forward.

But already the flames had narrowed the passage until there was hardly any room left.

Was he to die here with the horses, then?

He dug his heels harder in Cloudy's side and let out a yell that spurred the blinded horse forward even faster.

At last they were leaping past the tongues of fire. Out of the fire's mouth.

Into the fresh air.

Behind him, Carl Lee heard a crash and the beams of the barn came thundering down.

He could not get back into the barn to rescue the others.

He and Cloudy circled up and down in front of the barn, agony streaming down Carl Lee's face, and Cloudy still screaming.

"If only I'd had more time. If only I hadn't stopped to horse around with my friends I'd have caught that bum and saved the horses," he said to his grandfather as the firemen with their long hoses swished water on the flames.

Now he and Gray stood on each side of Cloudy rubbing the shivering Appaloosa, smelling the stench of burnt horse flesh, helpless as they listened for the silenced voices of the screamless horses trapped inside.

THE HIRED CARPENTERS, OVERSEEN BY CARL Lee, had raised the last hammer and rung the last nail into the last plank on the new barn.

"You've done a good job, my young contractor," Gray said to Carl Lee standing back looking at the new structure. "We won't worry about the outside painting yet, we'll get to it next summer, the wood preservative staining the panels will have to do for now."

"I'm wondering something, Grandpa," Carl Lee said as he hauled a bale of hay to the new stable. "Can you ever get a horse used to fire?"

"I doubt it," said Gray nervously fingering the letter Carl Lee had brought up from the mailbox.

"But I thought you said anything was possible."

"It is. But fear's powerful. We don't easily go against our instincts. And that's a truer truth for animals."

"But if a horse could get used to fire. . . . "

"It would save a lot of horse lives. As you yourself witnessed they panic because they can't shut their eyes and run on through fire to safety," said Gray.

"Yes," said Carl Lee remembering, "they trample each other. And then they get burnt up."

Carl Lee wondered about the ugly bum who started the fire.

"I guess that bum's far away from here by now," he said.

"If I catch him anywhere near this ranch, I'll fill his behind full of buckshot," Gray said angrily tearing open the letter.

Carl Lee braced himself for his father's message. Was this letter the most threatening, the most cruel letter of all? What was inside? Would his father forbid him to ride in the rodeo?

Gray read out loud quickly.

"Dear Papa, I'll see you both at the Boley Rodeo. I won't be able to visit you all after the event. I have to be to work the next day. But I'll pick up Carl Lee the Sunday before Attucks School starts as agreed. Your son, Samuel."

"Well now," said Gray. "Your daddy hasn't been to the rodeo in a long time."

Carl Lee barely heard his grandfather he was so busy trying to figure out the letter. He thought, It's not a threatening letter. Still you could never tell about Samuel. He often promised one thing and did another. Samuel might come to the rodeo drunk. And then he'd forget any promise he had made. Carl Lee prayed he'd show up sober.

Every day Carl Lee rode Cloudy. Then he would run beside him so fast until he could compete with the horse for speed. He thought about horses and fire and the additional pressure of having his father a spectator. Would what he did please his father? Or would he be the laughingstock of the event with his father laughing the loudest?

Running as fast as a horse was the first part of the performance he wanted to give at the rodeo.

But he had a feeling it wouldn't be enough. Wouldn't be spectacular enough.

The rodeo was a rough, rough place. A place where life and limb could be lost so easily. A place where ambulance sirens screamed and reputations were made and broken in a swirling second of hot clay dust and ice-cold sweat.

And the cowboys and rodeo fans were tough judges. They were used to the wonderful, the exciting.

It would take something quite extraordinary to get rodeo fans up out of their wooden seats.

Otherwise why take up space in the schedule of events?

He wanted to do something so wonderful even his hard to please father would applaud.

Carl Lee thought about all these things as he raked straw and toted buckets of water to the horses and cows.

After his chores were finished, he sat on a bale of hay thinking, his head bent and supported by one hand, looking like his own grandfather.

Thinking, thinking, thinking.

AUGUST CONTINUED TO BLAZE A TRAIL ACROSS the meadow. The August sun touched the tips of alfalfa grasses and buffalo weeds, turning them into hay.

When Carl Lee ran beside Cloudy he sometimes sent fox squirrels, minks, rabbits, raccoons and possums scurrying in the August woods. Watching from their branches or winging through the sky, the chee-chees scolded and starlings twittered until they sang the lightning bugs out at dusk. The lightning bugs flitted, glowing green, and winked at the boy and the horse practicing way past dusk beneath the country sky.

On many evenings after it was too late to ride Cloudy and run beside him, Gray found Carl Lee sitting on that bale of hay thinking with the barn light on. Then late one night he went into the barn and Carl Lee was up off the bale of hay working away at something.

"Kind of early for you to be in here, isn't it?" asked Gray. "Not practicing this midnight?"

"Later," said Carl Lee, carrying the joke further.

"What are you making with that leather, horse?" asked Gray. He was standing in the barn door opening, the

113

full moon glinting off his shoulders, watching Carl Lee snip and cut intently, concentrating on his work.

"I'm making some sunglasses for my horse," Carl Lee answered.

Gray chuckled. "I like your sense of humor."

But he noticed Carl Lee wasn't laughing, he was taking another piece of leather down from the barn wall and measuring it.

"But why are you doing this?" Gray asked.

"To find a way through fear," said Carl Lee, looking up from his work.

My goodness, thought Gray, he's grown over the summer. I think he's at least three feet taller. And talking more manly.

"Well, it won't be long before the sun is up. Better come in soon and get some rest," said Gray, just before walking back toward the house.

Many evenings, Gray stood on his porch and watched Carl Lee and Cloudy practicing in the field. The boy sometimes running alongside the horse.

Today his friend, Billingsley, joined him. "Why that's the most fleet-footed boy I ever saw," said Billingsley watching the boy and the horse running, riding and playing in the pasture.

"Won't be long before rodeo time," said Gray.

"Will he make it?" asked Billingsley.

Gray shrugged. "I keep telling him I don't know, but we'll see."

Soon it was a week before the rodeo and Carl Lee thought he was ready.

He brought out the horse blinders and showed Gray his stunt, perfectly timed so that with a flick of his wrist he released the blinders to cover the horse's eyes at just the right moment.

He had been extraordinarily careful, he had to be doubly careful not to let the horse get hurt.

"But how?" asked Gray, amazed.

"Practice, Grandpa."

"Do it again," he asked.

Again, Carl Lee and Cloudy performed the stunt. When he was sure Carl Lee could do it over and over again, as many times as he and Cloudy chose, Gray tossed his hat into the air and let out a great yell of joy.

"Cowboy!" Gray hollered. "It's rodeo time!"

RODEO

FROM THE CAB OF THE PICKUP CARL LEE could barely make out the outline of Cloudy riding quietly in the green trailer behind them as they jostled along the road to Boley.

Gray was quiet too, thinking.

Carl Lee followed suit, gazing out the window at the redbud trees and counting the miles from Golden Pasture to the rodeo and wondering if he would still be a cowpoke when the day was over. Or if he'd be a cowboy recognized by the small world of rodeo people.

Finally, he saw the sign proclaiming "Boley, Oklahoma, population 512."

"Not on Rodeo Day," he whispered; on Rodeo Day the population ran into the thousands.

The town wasn't big enough to hold all the spectators and participants, so the dusty campers spilled out into the countryside.

He read the license plates from Kansas, Texas, Arkansas, California and New York.

"Made it in good time," said Gray.

They pulled into the grounds at the same time as the rodeo clown was parking his truck.

The clown, already in makeup, settled his spike-haired chartreuse wig on his head as he climbed out of his vehicle, a pair of itchy-looking neon-green underwear on for costume. He leaned over and tied the strings on a pair of red-and-orange-striped boots.

"Seems like it took us forever," said Carl Lee.

"That's because you're anxious. What if you had to come as far away as the clown?" his grandfather said maneuvering the truck along the rodeo drive.

"Where's that?"

"Comes from the place where Bill Pickett, the cowboy who invented bulldogging, is buried. A little place called White Eagle, Oklahoma."

"White Eagle? That's five miles outside Ponca City!"

"Uh-huh. Ponca City, the place you were born," said Gray nodding his head. "That makes the clown almost a home boy for you then, my young cowpoke."

"It's a small world," admitted Carl Lee.

"And getting smaller."

After they had unhitched the trailer within the rodeo compound, they parked the truck in a line with the rest of the five-mile-long parade of cars, pickups and station wagons that had come to Boley especially for the rodeo.

Excitement was in the air. People lolling on hoods and fenders. A glad wail of music caught them in the act of wagging their heads.

Men in broken-down straw hats barbecued ribs and rabbits next to their cars and trucks, drinking that Red Mule and White Lightning, hollering at one another across smoke and husky slurred laughter.

Pecan Street. The main street in Boley. Barbecue stands and fish stands as far as Carl Lee could see.

119

"Hey man, you riding Broken Bones today?" the green-haired rodeo clown, adjusting the baggy pants of his lime green underwear, hollered.

The snaggle-toothed cowboy grinned. He had been taken out on a stretcher one famous year by Broken Bones when the newly arrived mustang, wild from the Oklahoma hills, wrecked a row of cars lined up near the rodeo fence, then broke the railing on the rider. Broken Bones had given him amnesia. The first thing the cowboy had said when he woke up in the hospital was this: "What happened?"

"Hey man, what happened?" a tobacco-spitting cowboy in a stained felt hat asked the unfortunate rider, slapping his leather chaps.

Hoorahing, is what Gray would call it. Fortunately the rider had recovered fully, else hoorahing would be out.

Harmless joking. Never see a fight, people just hanging out, having too much fun and eating each other's food in generous samples. Spiced with good-natured joking:

"How do I know what you're giving me is coon or not. Look like dog to me!"

"This ain't no dog. This here's barbecued coon. Still got his foot on him for proof. See here." And the man examined the coon's foot, satisfied. "Hey, Gray, you and your grandson wrap your lips around some of this here coon. Want the foot?"

As Carl Lee and Gray walked the five miles to the rodeo chutes they stopped often, tasting other Oklahoma recipes of barbecued coon, frog legs, catfish steaks, roasted goat and garfish.

Through it all, there was talk of the latest horses

brought in from the Oklahoma hills. "I'm just itching to break in Time Bomb."

"Either him or Knock Out."

"Give me Thunderfoot in the 'rena any rodeo day. I'd swop every bad bronc in the bunch for just one chance to bust that sonofagun."

"Yeah, but he ain't here."

Everywhere they stopped the cowboys were raising plenty of hell in peace.

As they neared the rodeo arena Carl Lee eyed the ambulances lined up outside the fence, ready to take hurt cowboys away. Would he end up in an ambulance like the man they hoorahed about "What happened?"

Outside the chutes, fenced in by weather-eaten wooden slats, cracked in places, he led Cloudy out of the horse trailer, rubbed him down, brushed his coat until it shone, then he laid the special blanket on the Appaloosa's back.

He stayed near his horse in the chute, listening to the other horses kicking in hollow bangs inside their small stables.

Soon most of the milling people had entered the grandstand and taken their wooden seats. Other spectators clustered around the outside of the fence ringing the arena. But Carl Lee did not see his father.

All through the hot day ranchers, cowboys, cowgirls, wives, husbands and cowpokes watched triumph and rodeo disgrace as cowboys left the arena, arms upheld in victory or taken out on stretchers.

Through the dust in the arena, Carl Lee could see the sunbeams dying in the powdery particles; he looked up and saw the sun hanging red and low over the grandstand. It was getting to be evening and Carl Lee's own test was nearing. His father had not shown up. He didn't know if he felt relieved or sad. At times both. Relieved that Samuel hadn't arrived ranting and raving drunk to stop him from performing. And sad that his father would not be there to cheer him on.

"Bulldogging!" the loudspeaker clacked. The noise escalated, the bulldoggers stood three feet deep at the ready. The wooden booths were jam-packed with grinning, joy-drinking men in straw hats.

These were the riders who rode in the bulldogging tradition of Bill Pickett. Riding alongside the bull, then diving on him. Catching the bull by the horn and twisting his head, taking him on down to the ground. Biting the dust.

The bulls snorted, lunged their thick heads, hurtling men through the air, eliminating cowboy after cowboy until there was only one left in the ring to confront the rankest bull in the stadium.

The rankest bull in the rodeo cannonballed out of a chute near Carl Lee. Rolled his great, fantastic eyes, wicked and red. Shook his head full of horns scored by scars.

The cowboy, shadowing the bull with his horse, finally made the dive, leaped aboard the bull's back, grabbed the awful horns, and held on.

"Go, man! Look at that cowboy handle that bull!"

"Go, man!"

The crowd roared the bulldogger on. He stayed clamped to the bucking back, his free arm raised.

The bull twisted in spirals, soaring upward, then plunging to the earth, still wheeling.

Then the cowboy was over the hump of the bull, working with the horns, then riding him on down to the earth. The bull was beat. The clowns caught the bull's attention. And the cowboy was home free.

Carl Lee looked all over the stadium, but his father was not there.

"Wild horses couldn't pull me away from here," a rodeo fan said, taking a swig of his corn whiskey and leaning out of his wooden booth.

"Quit drinking too much tanglefeet. What you think that is?" asked his partner when a New Mexico wild horse busted through the chute.

"Straight from the mountains, they didn't stop to wipe the dust off his withers. Look-a there. Horse still got the mountain mud on his hoofs. What? What's he doing? Kicked the saddle out of the rider's hand? A cowboy-maker. A cowboy-breaker.

"Look at him go, acting like Thunderfoot."

"He can go, but that ain't Thunderfoot."

"Ain't nobody crazy. We know Thunderfoot when we see him."

Gray cleared his throat, turned his head, looking up at the sky.

The man, still sipping at his fire water or tanglefeet as his partner called it, said, "Remember the year Thunderfoot sent ten men to the hospital. Sirens sounded like one long song."

Carl Lee could make out Billingsley sitting over in his jam-packed wooden booth, leaning across the railing, studying every move the horse made. Now and then he would look over at Gray and nod or shake his head.

Just then, Carl Lee saw his father enter the row on

123

which Billingsley sat and sit next to the older man. He looked . . . sober!

"Look, Grandpa, Daddy made it."

Gray looked over to the stand where Samuel sat and said, "The last time your daddy came to the rodeo was the night he saved Thunderfoot."

There was a huskiness to Gray's voice and a wistfulness as he looked over at Samuel. . . .

Then Gray followed Carl Lee's gaze back to the arena. The wild mustang couldn't be tamed; he bucked, he fought, knocked the horseman off and laid on his own back, kicking up his thrashing four legs and screaming the way wild horses scream. As if to say, come near me, you son of a buzzard, and I'll kill you.

The Boley cowboy was not frightened; brazened with bravery he tried the horse again and succeeded in mounting him. The horse broke out running, bucking, jerking, twisting and turning, trying to rid itself of the determined cowboy.

The wild horse whipped that cowboy from side to side. But even though his hat fell off his head, he stayed on, swaying with each thrust. All of a sudden the horse skidded to a stop, threw his thick neck back with such force, he catapulted the cowboy sending him sailing through the sky, head first, toward the grandstand. Looked like the horse took wings as he galloped away leaving a red plume of dust behind him.

The cowboy landed so hard he forgot to roll. He toppled to the ground with one foot folded up under him.

"Another two-legged pedigree bit the dust," somebody in the crowd hollered. Broke his leg.

Somebody must have told the ambulance driver, because the siren started before the cowboy had hit the ground good. At least it seemed that way to Carl Lee who grimaced as he watched the ambulance attendants running out of the arena with the injured cowboy on a stretcher.

I wouldn't want to be in his boots, Carl Lee thought.

"Can't ride bucking horses like we used to in the old days," grunted a bowlegged cowboy, a Camel cigarette sagging out of one corner of his wrinkled mouth. Outlined against the full moon, he looked like a walking raven.

The whistle blew.

Then it was Carl Lee's turn. He cinched the Appaloosa, setting the saddle high on his withers, then led him through the chute.

Carl Lee stroked the Appaloosa's long ears, which pointed and twitched as the horse listened to Carl Lee's encouraging whispers.

The crowd, led by his father's bass voice, was saying something Carl Lee couldn't make out. Perhaps, he thought, they're admiring the horse's saddle blanket covered with silver stars that Carl Lee had stitched.

Of course there was much to admire. Carl Lee had banded his blackberry hair with brilliant drake feathers fished from Opal Lake, and his cowboy shirt sparkled too, decorated as it was with the same spangle of stars patterned on Cloudy's saddle.

As the cowboys and cowgirls called and hooted in the stands, the aged and experienced rodeo hands hung around the sidelines, talking among themselves about the possible hazards of allowing a twelve-year-old to ride in the rodeo.

125

"I tell you that's got to be the horse. Only one like him in the world."

"It can't be, but it sure in hell looks like him."

"That kid might fall off and break his neck, I don't care if he is Gray's grand."

"Well," one man said slow as a mule tired from a two-day haul, "I bound you if he's Gray's grandchild he must be pedigree."

"Even thoroughbreds have to be groomed. What I want to know is, is the boy groomed yet? Especially for a horse like that?"

"What's he gonna do, cry if he fall?"

The old hands couldn't tell anything by studying Gray's face. He was so still, you would have thought God was breathing on him.

When Carl Lee finished whispering to Cloudy he stepped away from the horse, crouched down on the ground beside him, balanced forward on his toes, feet splayed, ready to sprint.

Then he called, "Cloudy!"

And the horse was a cloudy, bright sky of movement, a graceful arc of rhythm moving down the path. Carl Lee ran beside the horse like a night sky in liquid motion, the fringes of his leather pants flapping behind. The mane of Cloudy flying in the wind like a flag of freedom or liberty or something grand that horses are proud of.

Running. You could see the horse in Carl Lee.

Running. You could see Carl Lee in the Appaloosa.

The people had never seen anything like it before. A man-boy who could run as fast as a horse. A horse in rhythm with the boy.

Running, they reached the end of the corral and spun around, still running, in a circle, in unison, a dance between a boy and a horse.

Turning on the last beat, Carl Lee leaped onto Cloudy's back, secured his feet in the stirrups and without pause raced toward the place where Gray stood waiting at the end of the stadium.

This time as Carl Lee rode Cloudy it was as though they flew, melded together. When Carl Lee turned his head to the left, so did the horse. This turning was a signal to Gray to light the circle of fire.

An "O-O-O!" went up from the crowd as the design of fire, in the shape of a star, blazed over the dusky rodeo just as the lights in the stadium went out.

For a moment the astonished onlookers were quiet.

"Cloudy!" the boy yelled.

"Cowboy!" the crowd shouted in one great wave of sound.

"Cowboy!" called Gray.

Moving down the path straight to the jagged hoop of fire, Carl Lee pulled the blinders over the horse's eyes.

At just the right moment, he whispered in the horse's ear, "Jump!"

The crowd held its breath.

Then in one mighty leap, like a cloud or some other water image of a boy and a horse, they penetrated the flame.

Cheers engulfed the stadium as Carl Lee and Cloudy emerged unscathed on the other side of fire.

The doubting old hands took in the whole picture: the boy with feathers in his blackberry hair and his horse standing with a ray of light from the first evening star showering down on them, outlining a stage of dust and dirt enhanced by a natural spotlight.

The spotlight was an illumination emerging from a cloud, the star displayed the pair, the boy and his horse, in radiance.

Even Gray had lost his inscrutable expression as he observed the way the night star showered sparkles over the trembling horse and the victorious boy with the band of drake feathers around his head, holding the reins with his right hand, waving triumph to the applauding people with his left hand.

Gray seemed to be the only one in the stadium who heard thunder far away.

As Carl Lee reigned in his moment of glory, he spied a fan slouched over in the same pew as his father. The stranger was about six seats away from Samuel. Something about the man. . . . The shrouded posture. Cunning, like a fox. Treacherous. Up to no good. Hunched over under a raggedy cloak of evil.

Staring at the man, Carl Lee felt a spur in his chest. A light rain began to fall.

He started to turn away from looking, but the imaginary spur stung him again. And by reflex his mouth opened trying to figure something out as the rain swept down harder. He looked through the curtain of rain. And then he knew. Why that's who that is. It's the bum! The bum who started the fire!

The yellow-eyed man raised up slowly out of his seat.

"Father!" Carl Lee shouted.

Now the rain beat a noisy pattern. He repeated his shout, "Father!"

And his father heard him and followed Carl Lee's pointed finger.

Samuel stood up and got a good look at the terrible cowboy.

"Hellhound!" Samuel bellowed.

Hellhound turned, recognized Samuel and hesitated, looking from Samuel to Carl Lee's horse.

Hellhound waved something in his hand. Pointed it first at Samuel, then at the horse, trying to decide which to aim at first. He ranted, "I told you I'd find him! I'll kill that varmint for sure this time." And coming to a decision, he aimed a silver pistol at the horse.

The arena full of fans quieted. Nobody said a mumbling word. Nothing stirred in the danger-charged air except the innocent drone of falling rain.

A shot rang out.

A bullet whizzed past Carl Lee's nose. As he ducked, he saw his father leaping across the bleachers, intent on stopping Hellhound.

Slippery with rain, Hellhound slid out of Samuel's grasp and aimed again.

This time there was nobody to stop him. Samuel couldn't move fast enough.

Then the sky thundered with the sounds of the hoofs of a thousand phantom horses stampeding overhead. Light swept the darkness.

A bolt of lightning shot out of the sky and struck Hellhound so hard, it knocked the boots off his feet. A barefooted dead man tumbled into the arena and lay there, his burnt mouth filling with sloshing rain.

It was as though the creative hand of God reached

out of the sky and scratched Hellhound off the face of His world.

As Carl Lee saw the ambulance attendants dragging Hellhound off the arena he realized what the crowd had been yelling when he first brought Cloudy out of the chute and excitement had deafened his hearing. They had been screaming, "Thunderfoot!"

"Thunderfoot?!" So that was it, he realized as the rain started to fall in torrents. Their love of this one horse had brought them all, Carl Lee, Samuel and Gray, together.

Now, as the rain poured harder, his father and Gray helped him dismount.

His father shook his hand as they stood by the horse Carl Lee knew as Cloudy and his father knew as Thunderfoot.

In a look that spoke louder than words, Carl Lee's eyes echoed, man to man:

"Now we have ridden and freed the high spirit of the same horse. Up and down the world we have come."

When Carl Lee caught Samuel's rare smile, he thought, *He's listening to me*. The glow in Samuel's eyes reminded him of the light jumping in and out of the crystal stream. An opal flashed in Carl Lee's chest,. and he saw himself forever holding a horse's reins, leaning over the waters running clear and free through Opal Lake, and picking up the brilliant feathers of a heritage.

From the feathers, from his fathers, iridescent and grand, he would memorize the man texture and the male colors for all his years to come.

HORSES AND MEN

CARL LEE AND GRAY WERE RIDING HOME.

"Why didn't you tell me about Thunderfoot?" asked Carl Lee.

"I thought your father should tell you," answered Gray.

"So why didn't he tell me?"

"Because he's an angry man."

"But why?"

"Because I told you. Samuel's like that horse. He's been fenced in. Someday he'll find his spirit again just like Thunderfoot did with you."

THE GOLDEN WITNESS

A HARVEST OF OAK LEAVES BLEW STEADILY across the alfalfa fields. Some fell into Opal Lake and floated like big bright butterflies in the stream.

Samuel stopped his car to look out over the pasture strewn with autumn leaves. Then he continued driving along the dirt path leading to the ranch. He was coming to fetch his son and take him home to Ponca City.

He parked his car and walked across the wiregrass path. He listened to the sound of the yellowed leaves from the redbud tree crunching under his feet. A cow mooed patiently somewhere in the pasture. A tamed horse whinnied down by the stables.

Then, as though dropped out of the sky by a golden spirit, a solitary leaf touched his cheek and continued its flight to the ground.

Now he was beneath the southern pine trees where the summer sun bowed its head and waited for fall.

Today he was sober. Today his heart was steady. He put his hand on his father's door and entered the house.

At the desk in his room, Carl Lee waited, his packed suitcase on the bed. He looked out the window and

134

studied the trembling leaves, so orange they looked as if they had been kissed by fire.

"September's come to the golden pasture," he whispered.

It was time to say good-bye to Cloudy.

It was time to talk farewell words to Gray.

It was time to go back to Ponca City. With the father who sometimes couldn't see the miracle standing right there in front of him. With the father who had once been a hero.

Carl Lee decided he would remember the best that his father had been, even though he realized there were sure to be a few difficult times ahead. Maybe hidden beneath a spirit as icy as an alfalfa field in winter, Samuel Jefferson, the one who saved Thunderfoot, had a soul as warm as a golden pasture in summer.

Carl Lee had crossed another threshold, knowing the world was full of summer and winter people. In winter he'd remember summer.

Looking out over the meadow, at the trees changing color, at the sky taking on new shapes of clouds and gathering the wind to its chest, Carl Lee wanted to linger there forever but he stirred, hearing footsteps falling, coming down the hall.

There were many things to remember. This summer he had become a man.

He had a heritage. A backbone.

He had Thunderfoot.

He had a grandfather who crowned him king of the horses.

He had a hero for a father.

The footsteps came closer, but he did not get up yet.

Something held him there for another moment. Then through the open window, down, down out of the open sky, over the fields and lake the sound descended.

As though whispered by a golden witness, he heard this, the faintest of echoes, fly in through the window:

"Safe passage, safe passage along life's journey."

And the sound sparkled, like an opal in his ear.

JOYCE CAROL THOMAS was born in Ponca City, Oklahoma, not too far from where *The Golden Pasture* takes place. She received national critical attention when her first novel, *Marked by Fire*, won the American Book Award, and she is now considered to be among the forefront of black American women writers.

Joyce Carol Thomas is a playwright and producer, as well as the author of five books of poetry and two other novels for young adults, *Bright Shadow* and *Water Girl*. She has been assistant professor of English at California State University and visiting associate professor at Purdue University. Currently she writes full-time in Berkeley, California, where she lives.